THE PERFECT HOUSE

BLAKE PIERCE

Blake Pierce is author of the bestselling RILEY PAGE mystery series, which includes fifteen books (and counting). Blake Pierce is also the author of the MACKENZIE WHITE mystery series, comprising nine books (and counting); of the AVERY BLACK mystery series, comprising six books; of the KERI LOCKE mystery series, comprising five books; of the MAKING OF RILEY PAIGE mystery series, comprising three books (and counting); of the KATE WISE mystery series, comprising four books (and counting); of the CHLOE FINE psychological suspense mystery, comprising three books (and counting); and of the JESSE HUNT psychological suspense thriller series, comprising three books (and counting).

ONCE GONE (a Riley Paige Mystery—Book #1), BEFORE HE KILLS (A Mackenzie White Mystery—Book 1), CAUSE TO KILL (An Avery Black Mystery—Book 1), A TRACE OF DEATH (A Keri Locke Mystery—Book 1), and WATCHING (The Making of Riley Paige—Book 1) are each available as a free download on Amazon!

An avid reader and lifelong fan of the mystery and thriller genres, Blake loves to hear from you, so please feel free to visit www.blakepierceauthor.com to learn more and stay in touch.

BOOKS BY BLAKE PIERCE

A JESSIE HUNT PSYCHOLOGICAL SUSPENSE SERIES
THE PERFECT WIFE (Book #1)
THE PERFECT BLOCK (Book #2)
THE PERFECT HOUSE (Book #3)
THE PERFECT SMILE (Book #4)

CHLOE FINE PSYCHOLOGICAL SUSPENSE SERIES
NEXT DOOR (Book #1)
A NEIGHBOR'S LIE (Book #2)
CUL DE SAC (Book #3)
SILENT NEIGHBOR (Book #4)

KATE WISE MYSTERY SERIES
IF SHE KNEW (Book #1)
IF SHE SAW (Book #2)
IF SHE RAN (Book #3)
IF SHE HID (Book #4)
IF SHE FLED (Book #5)

THE MAKING OF RILEY PAIGE SERIES
WATCHING (Book #1)
WAITING (Book #2)
LURING (Book #3)
TAKING (Book #4)

RILEY PAIGE MYSTERY SERIES
ONCE GONE (Book #1)
ONCE TAKEN (Book #2)
ONCE CRAVED (Book #3)
ONCE LURED (Book #4)
ONCE HUNTED (Book #5)
ONCE PINED (Book #6)
ONCE FORSAKEN (Book #7)
ONCE COLD (Book #8)
ONCE STALKED (Book #9)
ONCE LOST (Book #10)
ONCE BURIED (Book #11)
ONCE BOUND (Book #12)
ONCE TRAPPED (Book #13)
ONCE DORMANT (Book #14)
ONCE SHUNNED (Book #15)

MACKENZIE WHITE MYSTERY SERIES
BEFORE HE KILLS (Book #1)
BEFORE HE SEES (Book #2)
BEFORE HE COVETS (Book #3)
BEFORE HE TAKES (Book #4)
BEFORE HE NEEDS (Book #5)
BEFORE HE FEELS (Book #6)
BEFORE HE SINS (Book #7)
BEFORE HE HUNTS (Book #8)
BEFORE HE PREYS (Book #9)
BEFORE HE LONGS (Book #10)

BEFORE HE LAPSES (Book #11)
BEFORE HE ENVIES (Book #12)

AVERY BLACK MYSTERY SERIES
CAUSE TO KILL (Book #1)
CAUSE TO RUN (Book #2)
CAUSE TO HIDE (Book #3)
CAUSE TO FEAR (Book #4)
CAUSE TO SAVE (Book #5)
CAUSE TO DREAD (Book #6)

KERI LOCKE MYSTERY SERIES
A TRACE OF DEATH (Book #1)
A TRACE OF MUDER (Book #2)
A TRACE OF VICE (Book #3)
A TRACE OF CRIME (Book #4)
A TRACE OF HOPE (Book #5)

THE PERFECT HOUSE

(A Jessie Hunt Psychological Suspense Thriller—Book Three)

BLAKE PIERCE

TABLE OF CONTENTS

Chapter One · 1
Chapter Two · 7
Chapter Three · 16
Chapter Four · 19
Chapter Five · 24
Chapter Six · 31
Chapter Seven · 37
Chapter Eight · 42
Chapter Nine · 50
Chapter Ten · 57
Chapter Eleven · 60
Chapter Twelve · 66
Chapter Thirteen · 73
Chapter Fourteen · 77
Chapter Fifteen · 84
Chapter Sixteen · 89
Chapter Seventeen · 94
Chapter Eighteen · 99
Chapter Nineteen · 102
Chapter Twenty · 106
Chapter Twenty-One · 110
Chapter Twenty-Two · 114
Chapter Twenty Three · 120
Chapter Twenty Four · 125

Chapter Twenty Five · 131
Chapter Twenty Six · 137
Chapter Twenty Seven · 142
Chapter Twenty-Eight · 149
Chapter Twenty Nine · 153
Chapter Thirty · 157
Chapter Thirty One · 163
Chapter Thirty Two · 167
Chapter Thirty Three · 171
Chapter Thirty Four ·174
Chapter Thirty Five · 179
Chapter Thirty Six · 184
Chapter Thirty Seven · 190
Chapter Thirty Eight · 195
Chapter Thirty Nine · 200
Chapter Forty · 205
Chapter Forty One · 208

CHAPTER ONE

Eliza Longworth took a long sip of her coffee as she looked out over the Pacific Ocean, marveling at the view only steps from her bedroom. Sometimes she had to remind herself just how lucky she was.

Her friend of twenty-five years, Penelope Wooten, sat in the adjoining chaise lounge on the patio overlooking Los Liones Canyon. It was a relatively clear March day and in the distance Catalina Island was visible. Looking to her left, Eliza could see the gleaming towers of downtown Santa Monica.

It was mid-morning on Monday. The kids had been packed off to daycare and school and the rush hour traffic had subsided. The only thing the longtime friends had on the schedule until lunchtime was hanging out in Eliza's three-story hillside Pacific Palisades mansion. If she wasn't so blissed out at the moment, she might even start to feel a little guilty. But as the notion slipped into her brain, she immediately forced it out.

You'll have lots of time to stress later today. Just allow yourself this moment.

"Want a coffee refill?" Penny asked. "I need a potty break anyway."

"No thanks. I'm good for now," Eliza said, before adding with a mischievous grin, "By the way, you know you can call it a bathroom break when there are just adults around, right?"

Penny stuck her tongue out in response as she got up, unfolding her impossibly long legs from the chair like a giraffe getting up after a nap. Her long, lustrous blonde hair, so much more stylish than Eliza's shoulder-length light brown variety, was tied up in a fashionably utilitarian ponytail. She still looked like the runway fashion model she'd been for much of her twenties before she gave it up for an admittedly less exciting, but far less manic, life.

She headed inside, leaving Eliza alone with her thoughts. Almost immediately, despite her best efforts, her mind returned to their conversation from minutes earlier. She replayed it as if on a loop she couldn't turn off.

"Gray seems so distant lately," Eliza had said. "Our one priority was always to have family dinner with the kids. But since he made senior partner, he's had all these dinner meetings."

"I'm sure he's as frustrated as you are," Penny had assured her. "Once things settle down, you'll probably get back to your old routine."

"I can handle him being gone more. I get it. He's got more responsibility for the success of the firm now. But what bugs me is that he doesn't seem to have any sense of loss about it. He's never expressed regret that he has to miss out. I'm not even sure he notices."

"I'm sure he does, Lizzie," Penny had said. "He probably just feels guilty about it. Acknowledging what he's missing would make it that much worse. I bet he's blocking it out. I do that sometimes."

"Do what exactly?" Eliza asked.

"Pretend that something I'm doing in my life that's not really admirable is no big deal because admitting it *is* a big deal would just make me feel worse about it."

"What do you do that's so bad?" Eliza asked mockingly.

"Just last week I ate half a can of Pringles in one sitting, for one thing. And then I yelled at the kids for wanting ice cream as an afternoon snack. So there's that."

"You're right. You're a horrible person."

Penny stuck her tongue out before responding. Penny was big on sticking out her tongue.

"My point is, maybe he's not as oblivious as it seems. Have you considered counseling?"

"You know I don't believe in that crap. Besides, why should I see a therapist when I have you? Between Penny therapy and yoga, I'm set emotionally. Speaking of, are we still on for tomorrow morning at your place?"

"Absolutely."

Thinking about it now, all joking aside, maybe marriage counseling wasn't such a bad idea. Eliza knew that Penny and Colton went every other week and they seemed to be the stronger for it. If she did go, she knew at least her best friend wouldn't rub it in.

They'd had each other's back ever since they were in elementary school. She still remembered when Kelton Prew pulled her pigtails and Penny had kicked him in the shin. That was the first day of third grade. They'd been thick as thieves ever since.

They'd helped each other through countless struggles. Eliza had been there for Penny when she had her bout with bulimia in high school. In their sophomore year of college, Penny had been the one to convince her it was *not* just a bad date, but that Ray Houson had raped her.

Penny went with her to campus police and sat in the courtroom to offer moral support when she testified. And when the tennis coach wanted to drop her from the team and pull her scholarship because she was still struggling months later, Penny went to him and threatened to help her friend sue the bastard. Eliza stayed on the team and won conference player of the year as a junior.

When Eliza miscarried after trying to get pregnant for eighteen months, Penny came over every day until she was finally ready to crawl out of bed. And when Penny's older son, Colt Jr., was diagnosed with autism, it was Eliza who did weeks of research and found the school that finally helped him start thriving.

They'd been through so many battles together that they liked to call themselves the Westside Warriors, even if their husbands thought the name was ridiculous. So if Penny was suggesting she reconsider marriage counseling, maybe she should.

Eliza was pulled out of her thoughts by a ding on Penny's phone. She reached over and grabbed it, ready to let her friend know someone was reaching out. But when she saw the name on the text, she opened the message. It was from Gray Longworth, Eliza's husband. It read:

Can't wait 2 c u 2nite. I miss your scent. Three days without u is too long. I told Lizzie I have a partner's dinner. Same time & place, right?

Eliza put the phone down. Her head was suddenly swimming and she felt weak. The mug slipped from her hand, hit the ground, and shattered into dozens of ceramic shards.

Penny ran back outside.

"Everything okay?" she asked. "I heard something break."

She looked down at the mug with coffee splattered all around it, and then up at Eliza's stunned face.

"What is it?" she asked.

Eliza's eyes moved involuntarily to Penny's phone and she watched her friend track them with her own. She saw the moment of recognition in Penelope's eyes as she put two and two together and realized what must have so startled her oldest, dearest friend.

"It's not like it seems," Penny said anxiously, dispensing with any attempt to deny what they both knew.

"How could you?" Eliza demanded, barely able to get the words out. "I trusted you more than anyone in the world. And you do this?"

She felt like someone had opened a trap door below her and she was falling into a pit of nothingness. Everything that grounded her life seemed to be disintegrating before her eyes. She thought she might throw up.

"Please, Eliza," Penny begged, kneeling down beside her friend. "Let me explain. It did happen, but it was a mistake—one that I've been trying to fix ever since."

"A mistake?" Eliza repeated, sitting upright in her chair as nausea mixed with anger, making a churning cauldron of bile bubble up from her stomach to her throat. "A mistake is tripping on a curb and knocking someone over. A mistake is forgetting to carry the one in a subtraction problem. A mistake isn't accidentally letting your best friend's husband inside you, Penny!"

"I know," Penny acknowledged, her voice choking with regret. "I shouldn't have said that. It was a terrible decision, made in a moment of weakness, fueled by too many glasses of viognier. I told him it was over."

"'Over' suggests it was more than once," Eliza noted, scrambling to her feet. "Exactly how long have you been sleeping with my husband?"

Penny stood there silently, clearly debating whether being honest would do more harm than good.

"About a month," she finally admitted.

Suddenly her husband's recent time away from the family made more sense. Each new revelation seemed to pack a new punch to the gut. Eliza felt that the only thing keeping her from collapsing was her sense of righteous rage.

"Funny," Eliza pointed out bitterly. "That's about how long Gray has been having those late-night partner meetings you told me he probably felt bad about. What a coincidence."

"I thought I could control it…" Penny started to say.

"Don't give me that," Eliza said, shutting her down. "We both know you can get restless. But this is how you dealt with it?"

"I know this doesn't help," Penny insisted. "But I was going to break it off. I haven't talked to him in three days. I was just trying to find a way to end it with him without blowing things up with you."

"Looks like you're going to need a new plan," Eliza spat, fighting the urge to kick the coffee cup shards at her friend. Only her bare feet prevented her. She clung to her anger, knowing it was the only thing keeping her from falling apart completely.

"Please, let me find a way to make this right. There has to be something I can do."

"There is," Eliza assured her. "Leave now."

Her friend stared at her for a moment. But she must have sensed how serious Eliza was because her hesitation was brief.

"Okay," Penny said, picking up her things and scurrying toward the front door. "I'll go. But let's talk later. We've been through so much together, Lizzie. Let's not let this ruin everything."

Eliza forced herself not to scream epithets in response. This might be the last time she ever saw her "friend" again and she needed her to understand the magnitude of the situation.

"This is different," she said slowly, with emphasis on each word. "All those other times were us against the world, having each other's back. This time you stabbed me in mine. Our friendship is over."

Then she slammed the door in her best friend's face.

CHAPTER TWO

Jessie Hunt woke up with a start, briefly unsure where she was. It took a moment to remember that she was in midair, on a Monday morning flight from Washington, D.C., back to Los Angeles. She looked at her watch and saw she still had two hours left before they landed.

Trying not to drift off again, she roused herself by taking a sip from the water bottle stuffed in the seatback pocket. She swished it around her mouth, trying to get rid of the cottonmouth coating her tongue.

She had good reason to nap. The last ten weeks had been among the most exhausting of her life. She had just completed the FBI's National Academy, an intense training program for local law enforcement personnel designed to familiarize them with FBI investigative techniques.

The exclusive program was only available to those nominated to attend by their supervisors. Unless accepted to go to Quantico to become a formal FBI agent, this crash course was the next best thing.

Under normal circumstances, Jessie wouldn't have been eligible to go. Until recently, she had only been an interim junior criminal profiling consultant for the LAPD. But after she solved a high-profile case, her stock had risen rapidly.

In retrospect, Jessie understood why the academy preferred more experienced officers. For the first two weeks of the program, she'd felt completely overwhelmed by the sheer volume of information being thrown at her. She had classes in forensic science, law, terrorist mindsets, and her area of focus, behavioral science, which emphasized getting inside the minds of killers to better understand their motives. And none of that included the relentless physical training that left every muscle aching.

Eventually, she found her bearings. The courses, which were reminiscent of her recent graduate work in criminal psychology, began to make sense. After about a month, her body was no longer screaming when she woke up each morning. And best of all, the time she spent in the Behavioral Sciences Unit allowed her to interact with the best serial killer experts in the world. She hoped to one day be among them.

There was one added benefit. Because she worked so hard, both mentally and physically, for almost every waking moment, she hardly ever dreamed. Or at least, she didn't have nightmares.

Back home, she often woke up screaming in a cold sweat as memories of her childhood or her more recent traumas replayed in her unconscious. She still remembered her most recent source of anxiety. It was her last conversation with incarcerated serial killer Bolton Crutchfield, the one in which he'd told her he would be chatting with her own murderous father sometime soon.

If she had been back in L.A. for the last ten weeks, she'd have spent most of that time obsessing over whether Crutchfield was telling the truth or screwing with her. And if he *was* being honest, how would he manage to coordinate a discussion with an on-the-lam killer while he was being held in a secure mental hospital?

But because she'd been thousands of miles away, focused on unrelentingly challenging tasks for almost every waking second, she hadn't been able to fixate on Crutchfield's claims. She likely would again soon, but not just yet. Right now, she was simply too tired for her brain to mess with her.

As she settled back into her seat, allowing sleep to envelop her again, Jessie had a thought.

So all I have to do to get good sleep for the rest of my life is spend every morning working out until I almost throw up, followed by ten hours of non-stop professional instruction. Sounds like a plan.

Before she fully formed the grin that was beginning to play at her lips, she was asleep again.

That sense of cozy comfort disappeared the second she walked outside of LAX just after noon. From this moment on, she would need to be on constant guard again. After all, as she'd learned before she left for Quantico, a never-captured serial killer was on the hunt. Xander Thurman had been looking for her for months. Thurman also happened to be her father.

She took a rideshare from the airport to work, which was the Central Community Police Station in downtown L.A. She didn't formally start work again until tomorrow and wasn't in the mood to chat, so she didn't even go into the main bullpen of the station.

Instead, she went to her assigned mailbox cubby and collected her mail, which had been forwarded from a post office box. No one—not her work colleagues, not her friends, not even her adoptive parents—knew her actual address. She'd rented the apartment through a leasing company; her name was nowhere on the agreement and there was no paperwork connecting her to the building.

Once she grabbed the mail, she walked along a side corridor to the motor pool, where taxis were always waiting in the adjoining alley. She hopped in one and directed it to the retail strip center that was situated next to her apartment complex, about two miles away.

One reason she'd picked this place to live after her friend Lacy had insisted she move out was that it was difficult to find and even harder to access without permission. First of all, its parking structure was under the adjoining retail complex in the same building, so anyone following her would have a hard time determining where she was going.

Even if someone did figure it out, the building had a doorman and a security guard. The front door and the elevators both required keycards. And none of the apartments themselves had unit numbers listed on the outside. Residents just had to remember which was theirs.

Still, Jessie took extra precautions. Once the cab, which she paid for with cash, dropped her off, she walked into the retail center. First she passed quickly through a coffee shop, meandering through the crowd before taking a side exit.

Then, pulling the hood of her sweatshirt over her shoulder-length brown hair, she passed through a food court to a hallway that had restrooms next to a door marked "Employees Only." She pushed open the women's restroom door so that anyone following her would see it closing and think she'd gone in. Instead, not looking back, she hurried through the employee entrance, which was a long hallway with back door entrances to each business.

She jogged along the curved corridor until she found a stairwell with a sign marked "Maintenance." Hurrying down the steps as quietly as possible, she used the keycard she'd gotten from the building manager to unlock that door too. She'd negotiated special authorization to this area based on her LAPD connection rather than by trying to explain that her precautions were related to having an on-the-loose serial killer for a father.

The maintenance door closed and locked behind her as she navigated her way along a narrow passage with exposed pipes jutting out at all angles and metal cages securing equipment she didn't understand. After several minutes of dodging and weaving among the obstacles, she reached a small alcove near a large boiler.

Midway down the passage, the recessed area was unlit and easy to miss. She'd had to have it pointed out to her the first time she'd been down here. She stepped into the alcove as she pulled out the old key she'd been given. The lock to this door was an old-school bolt. She turned it, pushed open the heavy door, and quickly closed and locked it behind her.

Now in the supply room on the basement level of her apartment building, she had officially transitioned from the retail center property to the apartment complex. She hurried through the darkened room, nearly tripping over a tub of bleach lying on the floor. She opened that door, passed through the empty maintenance manager's office, and walked up the tight stairwell that opened onto the back hallway of the apartment building's main floor.

She rounded the corner to the vestibule with the bank of elevators, where she could hear Jimmy the doorman and Fred the security guard amiably chatting with a resident in the front lobby. She didn't have time to catch up with them now but promised herself she would reconnect later.

Both were nice guys. Fred was a former highway patrolman who had retired early after a bad on-the-job motorcycle accident. It left him with a limp and a large scar on his left cheek, but that didn't stop him from constantly joking around. Jimmy, in his mid-twenties, was a sweet, earnest kid using this job to pay his way through college.

She moved past the vestibule to the service elevator, which wasn't visible from the lobby, swiped her card, and waited anxiously to see if anyone had followed her. She knew the chances were remote but that didn't stop her from shifting nervously from one foot to the other until the elevator arrived.

When it did, she stepped in, pushed the button for the fourth floor, and then the one to close the door. When the doors opened, she scurried down the hall until she got to her apartment. Taking a moment to catch her breath, she studied her door.

On first glance, it looked as nondescript as all the others on the floor. But she'd had several security upgrades added when she moved in. First, she stepped back so that she was three feet away from the door and directly in line with the peephole. A dull green glow that wasn't visible from any other angle emanated from the rim around the hole, an indicator that the unit had not been forcibly accessed. Had it been, the rim around the peephole would have been red.

In addition to the Nest doorbell camera she'd had installed, there were also multiple hidden cameras in the corridor. One had a direct view of her door. Another focused on the hall facing back to the elevator and the adjoining stairwell. A third pointed in the other direction of the second set of stairs. She'd checked them all on the way over in the cab and found no suspicious movement around her place today.

The next step was entry. She used a traditional key to open one bolt, then swiped her card and heard the other sliding bolt open as well. She stepped inside as the motion sensor alarm warning went off, dropped her backpack on the floor, and ignored the alarm as she rebolted both doors and pulled the sliding security bar across as well. Only then did she punch in the eight-digit code.

After that she grabbed the nightstick she kept by the door and hurried to the bedroom. She lifted up the removable picture frame beside the light switch to reveal the hidden security panel and punched in the four-digit code for the second, silent alarm—the one that went straight to the police if she didn't deactivate it in forty seconds.

Only then did she allow herself to breathe. As she inhaled and exhaled slowly, she walked around the small apartment, nightstick in hand, ready for anything. Searching the whole place, including the closets, shower, and pantry, took under a minute.

When she was confident that she was alone and secure, she checked the half dozen nanny-cams she had placed throughout the unit. Then she evaluated the locks on the windows. Everything was in working order. That left only one place to review.

She stepped into the bathroom and opened the narrow closet that held shelves with supplies like extra toilet paper, a plunger, some bars of soap, shower scrubbers, and mirror cleaning fluid. There was a small clasp on the left side of the closet, not visible unless one knew where to look. She flipped it and tugged, feeling the hidden latch click.

The shelving unit swung open, revealing an extremely narrow shaft behind it, with a rope ladder attached to the brick wall. The tube and ladder extended from her fourth-floor unit down to a crawl space in the basement laundry room. It was designed as her last-ditch emergency exit if all her other security measures fell through. She hoped she'd never need it.

She replaced the shelf and was about to return to the living room when she caught sight of herself in the bathroom mirror. It was the first time she'd really studied herself at length since she left. She liked what she saw.

On the surface, she didn't look that different from before. She'd had a birthday while at the FBI and was now twenty-nine, but she didn't look older. In fact, she thought she looked better than when she'd left.

Her hair was still brown, but it seemed somehow bouncier, less limp than it had been when she left L.A. all those weeks ago. Despite the long days at the FBI, her green eyes sparkled with energy and no longer had the dark shadows underneath that had become so familiar to her. She was still a lean five feet ten, but she felt stronger and firmer than before. Her arms were more toned and her core was tight from endless sit-ups and planks. She felt... prepared.

Moving into the living room, she finally turned on the lights. It took her a second to remember that all the furniture in the space was hers. She'd bought most of it just before she'd left for Quantico. She hadn't had much choice. She'd sold all the stuff from the house she'd owned with her sociopathic, currently incarcerated ex-husband, Kyle. For a while after that, she crashed at the apartment of her old college friend, Lacy Cartwright. But after it was broken into by someone sending a message to Jessie on behalf of Bolton Crutchfield, Lacy had insisted she leave, pretty much right then.

So she'd done exactly that, living in a weekly hotel for a while until she found a place—this place—that met her security needs. But it was unfurnished, so she'd burned a chunk of her money from the divorce all at once on furniture and appliances. Since she'd had to leave for the National Academy so soon after buying it all, she hadn't gotten a chance to appreciate any of it.

Now she hoped to. She sat down on the love seat and leaned back, settling in. There was a cardboard box marked "stuff to go through" sitting on the floor beside her. She picked it up and began rifling through it. Most of it was paperwork she had no intention of dealing with now. At the very bottom of the box was an 8x10 wedding photo of her and Kyle.

She stared at it almost uncomprehendingly, amazed that the person who had that life was the one sitting here now. Almost a decade ago, during their sophomore year at USC, she'd started dating Kyle Voss. They'd moved in together soon after graduation and gotten married three years ago.

For a long time, things seemed great. They lived in a cool apartment not far from here in downtown Los Angeles, or DTLA as it was often called. Kyle had a good job in finance and Jessie was getting her master's degree. Their life was comfortable. They went to new restaurants and checked out the hot bars. Jessie was happy and probably could have stayed that way for a long time.

But then Kyle got a promotion at the company's office in Orange County and insisted they move to a McMansion there. Jessie had consented, despite her apprehension. It was only then that Kyle's true nature was revealed. He became obsessed with joining a secret club that turned out to be a front for a prostitution ring. He began an affair with one of the women there. And when it went bad, he killed her and tried to frame Jessie for it. To top it all off, when Jessie uncovered his plot, he tried to kill her too.

But even now, as she studied the wedding photo, there was no hint of what her husband was ultimately capable of. He looked like a handsome, amiable, rough-around-the-edges future master of the universe. She crumpled up the photo and tossed it toward the trash can in the kitchen. It dropped right in the center, giving her an unexpected cathartic rush.

Swish! That must mean something.

There was something freeing about this place. Everything—the new furniture, the lack of personal mementos, even the borderline paranoid security measures—belonged to *her*. She had a fresh start.

She stretched out, allowing her muscles to relax after the long flight on the tightly packed plane. This apartment was hers—the first place in over half a dozen years she could truly say that about. She could eat pizza on the couch and leave the box lying around without worrying about anyone complaining. Not that she was the type to do that. But the point was, *she could.*

The thought of pizza made her suddenly hungry. She got up and checked the fridge. Not only was it empty, it wasn't even turned on. Only then did she remember that she'd left it that way, not seeing any reason to pay for the electricity if she was going to be gone for two and a half months.

She plugged it in and, feeling restless, decided to make a grocery run. Then she had another idea. Since she didn't start work until tomorrow and it wasn't too late in the afternoon there was another stop she could make: a place—and a person—she knew she'd eventually have to visit.

She had managed to put it out of her head for most of her time at Quantico but there was still the matter of Bolton Crutchfield. She knew she should let it go, that he had been baiting her during their last meeting.

And yet she had to know: had Crutchfield really found a way to meet with her father, Xander Thurman, the Ozarks Executioner? Had he found a way to reach out to the murderer of countless people, including her mother; the man who left her, a six-year-old child, tied up next to the body to face certain death in a freezing, isolated cabin?

She was about to find out.

CHAPTER THREE

Eliza was waiting when Gray got home that night. He arrived in time for dinner, with a look on his face that suggested he knew what was coming. Since Millie and Henry were sitting right there eating their mac & cheese with hot dog slices, neither parent said anything about the situation.

It was only after the kids were down for the night that it came up. Eliza was standing in the kitchen when Gray walked in after putting them to sleep. He had taken off his sport coat but was still wearing his loosened tie and slacks. She suspected it was to make him look more credible.

Gray wasn't a big man. At five foot nine and 160 pounds he was only an inch taller than she was, though he outweighed her by a good thirty pounds. But they both knew that he was far less imposing in a T-shirt and sweatpants. Business attire was his armor.

"Before you say anything," he began, "please let me try to explain."

Eliza, who had spent much of the day turning over how this could have happened, was happy let her anguish take a temporary back seat and allow him to squirm as he tried to justify himself.

"Be my guest," she said.

"First. I'm sorry. No matter what else I say, I want you to know that I apologize. I should never have let it happen. It was a moment of weakness. She's known me for years and she knew my vulnerabilities, what would pique my interest. I should have known better but I fell for it."

"What are you saying?" Eliza asked, dumbfounded as much as hurt. "That Penny was some seductress who manipulated you into having an affair with her? We both know that you're a weak man, Gray, but are you kidding me?"

"No," he said, choosing not to respond to the "weak" comment. "I take full responsibility for my actions. I had the three whiskey sours. I ogled her legs in the dress with the slit up the side. But she knows what makes me tick. I guess it's all those heart-to-hearts you two have had over the years. She knew to brush her fingertip along my forearm. She knew to talk, almost purr in my left ear. She likely knew you hadn't done any of those things in a long time. And she knew you wouldn't be walking into that cocktail party because you were back home, knocked out on the sleeping pills you take most nights."

That hung in the air for several seconds as Eliza tried to compose herself. When she was sure she wouldn't yell, she replied in a shockingly quiet voice.

"Are you blaming me for this? Because it sounds like you're saying you couldn't keep it in your pants because I have trouble sleeping at night."

"No, I didn't mean it like that," he sniveled, backing down at the venom in her words. "It's just that you *always* have trouble sleeping at night. And you never seem all that interested in staying up with me."

"Just to be clear, Grayson—you say you're not blaming me. But then you immediately transition into saying I'm too knocked out on Valium and don't give you enough big boy attention, so you had to have sex with my best friend."

"What kind of best friend is she to do that anyway?" Gray tossed out desperately.

"Don't change the subject," she spat, forcing herself to keep her voice steady, partly to avoid waking the kids but mostly because doing so was the only thing keeping her from losing it. "She's already on my list. It's your turn now. You couldn't have come to me and said, 'Hey honey, I'd really love to spend a romantic evening with you tonight' or 'Sweetie, I feel disconnected from you lately. Can we get closer this evening?' Those weren't options?"

"I didn't want to wake you up to bother you with questions like that," he replied, his voice meek but his words cutting.

"So you've decided sarcasm is the way to go here?" she demanded.

"Look," he said, wriggling around for any way out, "it's over with Penny. She told me that this afternoon and I agreed. I don't know how we move past this but I want to, if only for the kids."

"If only for the kids?' she repeated, stunned at how many ways he could fail at once. "Just get out. I'm giving you five minutes to pack a bag and be in your car. Book a hotel until further notice."

"You're kicking me out of my own house?" he asked, disbelieving. "The house I paid for?"

"Not only am I kicking you out," she hissed, "if you're not pulling out of the driveway in five minutes, I'm calling the cops."

"To tell them what?"

"Try me," she seethed.

Gray stared at her. Undeterred, she walked over to the phone and picked it up. It was only when he heard the dial tone that he snapped into action. Within three minutes, he was scampering out the door like a dog with its tail between its legs, his duffel bag stuffed with dress shirts and jackets. A shoe fell out as he rushed toward the door. He didn't notice and Eliza didn't say anything.

It was only when she heard the car peel out that she put the phone back in its dock. She looked down at her left hand and saw that her palm was bleeding where she'd been digging her nails into it. Only now did she feel the sting.

CHAPTER FOUR

Despite being out of practice, Jessie navigated the traffic from downtown L.A. to Norwalk without too much trouble. Along the way, as a way to push her impending destination out of her mind, she decided to call her folks.

Her adoptive parents, Bruce and Janine Hunt, lived in Las Cruces, New Mexico. He was retired FBI and she was a retired teacher. Jessie had spent a few days with them on her way to Quantico and had hoped to do the same on the way back as well. But there wasn't enough time between the end of the program and her start back at work so she'd had to forgo the second visit. She hoped to return again soon, especially since her mom was battling cancer.

It didn't seem fair. Janine had been fighting it on and off for over a decade now and that was on top of the other tragedy they'd faced years ago. Just before they took Jessie in when she was six, they had lost their toddler son, also to cancer. They were eager to fill the void in their hearts, even if it meant adopting the daughter of a serial killer, one who had murdered her mother and left her for dead. Because Bruce was in the FBI, the fit seemed logical to the U.S. Marshals who had put Jessie in Witness Protection. On paper, it all made sense.

She forced that out of her head as she dialed their number.

"Hi, Pa," she said. "How's it going?"

"Okay," he answered. "Ma's napping. Do you want to call back later?"

"No. We can talk. I'll speak to her tonight or something. What's happening there?"

Four months ago, she would have been reluctant to speak to him without her mom there too. Bruce Hunt was a hard man to get close to and Jessie wasn't a ball of cuddliness either. Her memories of her youth with him were a mix of joy and frustration. There were ski trips, camping and hiking in the mountains, and family vacations to Mexico, only sixty miles away.

But there were also screaming matches, especially when she was a teenager. Bruce was a man who appreciated discipline. Jessie, with years of pent-up resentment over losing her mother, her name, and her home all at once, tended to act out. During her years at USC and after, they probably spoke less than two dozen times total. Visits back and forth were rare.

But recently, the return of Ma's cancer had forced them to speak without a middleman. And the ice had somehow broken. He'd even come out to L.A. to help her recuperate after her abdominal injury when Kyle attacked her last fall.

"Things are quiet here," he said, answering her question. "Ma had another chemo session yesterday, which is why she's recuperating now. If she feels well enough, we may go out for dinner later."

"With the whole cop crew?" she asked jokingly. A few months ago, her folks had moved from their home to a senior living facility populated primarily by retirees from the Las Cruces PD, Sheriff's Department, and FBI.

"Nah, just the two of us. I'm thinking a candlelit dinner. But somewhere where we can put a bucket beside the table in case she has to puke."

"You really are a romantic, Pa."

"I try. How are things with you? I'm assuming you passed the FBI training."

"Why do you assume that?"

"Because you knew I'd ask you about it and you wouldn't have called if you had to deliver bad news."

Jessie had to hand it to him. For an old dog, he was still pretty sharp.

"I passed," she assured him. "I'm back in L.A. now. I start work again tomorrow and I'm...out running errands."

She didn't want to worry him with her actual current destination.

"That sounds ominous. Why do I get the feeling you're not out shopping for a loaf of bread?"

"I didn't mean for it to sound like that. I guess I'm just wiped out from all the travel. I'm actually almost here," she lied. "Should I call back tonight or wait until tomorrow? I don't want to mess with your fancy, puke bucket dinner."

"Maybe tomorrow," he advised.

"Okay. Say hi to Ma. I love you."

"Love you too," he said, hanging up.

Jessie tried to focus on the road. The traffic was getting worse and the drive to the NRD facility, which took about forty-five minutes, still had a half hour left.

NRD, short for Non-Rehabilitative Division, was a special stand-alone unit affiliated with the Department State Hospital–Metropolitan in Norwalk. The main hospital was home to a wide array of mentally disordered perpetrators deemed unfit to serve time in a conventional prison.

But the NRD annex, unknown to the public and even to most law enforcement and mental health personnel, served a more clandestine role. It was designed to house a maximum of ten felons off the grid. Right now there were only five people being held there, all men, all serial rapists or killers. One of them was Bolton Crutchfield.

Jessie's mind wandered to the most recent time she'd been there to see him. It was her last visit before she left for the National Academy, though she hadn't told him that. Jessie had been visiting Crutchfield regularly ever since last fall, when she'd gotten permission to interview him as part of her master's practicum. According to the staff there, he almost never consented to talk to doctors or researchers. But for reasons that didn't become clear to her until later, he'd agreed to meet with her.

Over the next few weeks they came to a kind of agreement. He would discuss the particulars of his crimes, including methods and motives, if she shared some details of her own life. It seemed like a fair trade initially. After all, her goal was to become a criminal profiler specializing in serial killers. Having one willing to discuss the details of what he'd done could prove invaluable.

And there turned out to be an added bonus. Crutchfield had a Sherlock Holmesian ability to deduce information, even when locked in a cell in a mental hospital. He could discern details about Jessie's life at that moment just by looking at her.

He'd used that skill, along with case information she shared, to give her clues to several crimes, including the murder of a wealthy Hancock Park philanthropist. He'd also tipped her off that her own husband might not be as trustworthy as he seemed.

Unfortunately for Jessie, his skills at deduction also worked against her. The reason she'd wanted to meet with Crutchfield in the first place was because she'd noticed that he'd modeled his murders after those of her father, legendary, never-caught serial killer Xander Thurman. But Thurman committed his crimes in rural Missouri over two decades earlier. It seemed like a random, obscure choice for a Southern California–based killer.

But it turned out that Bolton was a big fan. And once Jessie started by asking him about his interest in those old murders, it didn't take him long to piece things together and determine that the young woman in front of him was personally connected to Thurman. Eventually he admitted that he knew she was his daughter. And he revealed one more tidbit—he'd met with her dad two years earlier.

With glee in his voice, he'd informed her that her father had entered the facility under the guise of a doctor and managed to have an extended conversation with the prisoner. Apparently he was looking for his daughter, whose name had been changed and who had been put in the Witness Protection Program after he killed her mother. He suspected that she might one day visit Crutchfield because their crimes were so similar. Thurman wanted Crutchfield to let him know if she ever showed up and give him her new name and location.

From that moment on, their relationship had an inequality that made her incredibly uncomfortable. Crutchfield still gave her information about his crimes and hints about others. But they both knew that he held all the cards.

He knew her new name. He knew what she looked like. He knew the city she lived in. At one point she discovered he even knew she'd been living at her friend Lacy's place and where that was. And apparently, despite being incarcerated in a supposedly secret facility, he had the capability of giving her father all those details.

Jessie was pretty sure that was at least part of the reason that Lacy, an aspiring fashion designer, had taken a six-month gig working in Milan. It was a great opportunity but it was also half a world away from Jessie's dangerous life.

As Jessie pulled off the freeway, only minutes from reaching NRD, she recalled how Crutchfield had finally pulled the trigger on the unspoken threat that had always hung over their meetings.

Maybe it was because he sensed she was leaving for several months. Maybe it was just out of spite. But the last time she'd looked through the glass into his devious eyes, he'd dropped a bombshell on her.

"I'll be having a little chat with your father," he'd told her in his courtly Southern accent. "I won't spoil things by saying when. But it's going to be lovely, I'm quite certain."

She had barely managed to choke out the word "How?"

"Oh, don't you worry about that, Miss Jessie," he'd said soothingly. "Just know that when we do talk, I'll be sure to give him your regards."

As she pulled onto the hospital property, she asked herself the same question that had been eating at her ever since, the one she could only put out of her head when she was intently focused on other work: had he really done it? While she was off learning how to catch people like him and her dad, had the two of them really met a second time, despite all the security precautions designed to prevent just that sort of thing?

She had a feeling that mystery was about to be solved.

CHAPTER FIVE

Entering the NRD unit was just as she'd remembered. After getting authorization to enter the enclosed hospital campus through a guard gate, she drove behind the main building to a second, smaller, nondescript one in the back.

It was a bland concrete and steel one-story structure in the middle of an unpaved parking lot. Only the roof was visible behind a large, green-meshed barbed-wire metal fence that surrounded the whole place.

She passed through a second guard gate to access NRD. After parking, she walked toward the main entrance, pretending to ignore the multiple security cameras that followed her every step. When she got to the exterior door, she waited to be buzzed in. Unlike the first time she'd come, she was now recognized by the staff and admitted on sight.

But that was only for the outer door. After passing through a small courtyard, she reached the main entrance to the facility, which had thick, bulletproof glass doors. She swiped her entry card, which made the panel light turn green. Then the security officer behind the desk inside, who could see the color change as well, buzzed her in, completing the entry process.

Jessie stood in a small vestibule, waiting for the outer door to close. Experience had taught her that the inner door couldn't be opened until the outer one shut completely. Once it locked audibly, the security guard unlocked the interior door.

Jessie stepped inside, where a second armed officer stood waiting for her. He collected her personal belongings, which were minimal. She'd learned over time that she was better off leaving almost everything in the car, which was in no danger of being broken into.

The guard patted her down and then motioned for her to go through the airport security-style millimeter wave scanner, which gave a detailed impression of her entire body. After she'd gone through, her items were returned without a word. It was the only indication that she was free to continue on.

"Is Officer Gentry meeting me?" she asked the officer behind the desk.

The woman looked up at her, an expression of complete disinterest on her face. "She'll be out in a moment. Just wait by the Transitional Prep door."

Jessie did as she was instructed. Transitional Prep was the room where all visitors went to change before interacting with a patient. Once inside, they were required to change into gray, hospital-style scrubs, remove all jewelry, and wash off any makeup. As she'd been warned, these men didn't need any additional stimulation.

A moment later, Officer Katherine "Kat" Gentry stepped out the prep door to greet her. She was a sight for sore eyes. Though they hadn't exactly gotten off on the right foot when they'd first met last summer, now the two women were friends, connected by a shared awareness of the darkness inside some people. Jessie had grown to trust her so much that Kat was one of fewer than a half dozen people in the world who knew she was the daughter of the Ozarks Executioner.

As Kat walked over, Jessie noted once again how much of a hard-ass NRD's head of security was. Physically imposing despite being an unexceptional five foot seven, her 140-pound body was comprised almost entirely of muscle and steel will. A former Army Ranger who'd served two tours in Afghanistan, she bore the remnants of those days on her face, which was pockmarked from shrapnel burns and had a long scar that started just below her left eye and ran vertically down the side of her cheek. Her gray eyes were measured, thoroughly taking in everything she saw to determine if it was a threat.

She clearly didn't consider Jessie one. She broke into a grin and gave her a big hug.

"Long time, no see, FBI lady," she said enthusiastically.

Jessie gasped for breath at the viselike embrace, only speaking once she was released.

"I'm not FBI," she reminded Kat. "It was just a training program. I'm still affiliated with LAPD."

"Whatever," Kat said dismissively. "You were at Quantico, working with the authorities in your field, learning fancy FBI techniques. If I want to call you an FBI lady, that's what I'll do."

"If it means you won't crack my spine in half, you can call me whatever you want."

"Speaking of, I don't think I could do that anymore," Kat noted. "You seem stronger than before. I'm guessing they didn't just work out your brain while you were there."

"Six days a week," Jessie told her. "Long trail runs, obstacle courses, self-defense, and weapons training. They definitely kicked my butt into halfway decent shape."

"Should I be worried?" Kat asked with faux concern, stepping back and lifting her arms into a defensive stance.

"I don't think I'm any threat to you," Jessie admitted. "But I do feel like I could protect myself around a suspect, which was definitely not the case before. Looking back, I was lucky to have survived a few of my recent encounters."

"That's awesome, Jessie," Kat said. "Maybe we should spar sometime, go a few rounds, just to keep you sharp."

"If by go a few rounds, you mean a few rounds of shots, I'm in. Otherwise, I may take a little break from the daily running and hitting and such."

"I take it all back," Kat said. "You're still the same wuss you always were."

"Now *that's* the Kat Gentry I've come to know and love. I knew there was a reason you were the first person I wanted to see when I got back in town."

"I'm flattered," Kat said. "But I think we both know I'm not the person you're really here to see. Should we stop stalling and head in?"

Jessie nodded and followed Kat into Transitional Prep, where the sterility and silence put an end to the visit's playful vibe.

Fifteen minutes later, Kat led Jessie to the door that connected to the NRD security wing to some of the most dangerous people on the planet. They'd already gone to her office for a debriefing about the last few months, which had been surprisingly uneventful.

Kat informed her that once Crutchfield had threatened an imminent meeting with her father, the already tight security had been increased even more. The facility added additional security cameras and even more identity verification for visitors.

There was no evidence that Xander Thurman had tried to visit Crutchfield. His only guests had been the doctor who came every month to check his vitals, the psychiatrist he almost never spoke to, an LAPD detective who hoped, futilely as it turned out, that Crutchfield would share info on a cold case he was working, and his court-appointed lawyer, who showed up only to make sure he wasn't being tortured. He barely engaged with any of them.

According to Kat, he hadn't mentioned Jessie to the staff, not even to Ernie Cortez, the easygoing officer who supervised his weekly showers. It was as if she didn't exist. She wondered if he was pissed at her.

"I know you remember the drill," Kat said, as they stood at the security door. "But it's been a few months so let's just review the security procedures as a precaution. Don't approach the prisoner. Don't touch the glass barrier. I know this one will get thrown out the window, but officially, you're not supposed to share any personal information. Got it?"

"Yep," Jessie said, happy for the reminders. It was helpful to get her in the proper frame of mind.

Kat swiped her badge and nodded at the camera over the door. Someone inside buzzed them in. Jessie was immediately overwhelmed by the surprising flurry of activity. Instead of the usual four security guards, there were six. In addition, there were three men in workmen uniforms walking around with various pieces of technical equipment.

"What's going on?" she asked.

"Oh, I forgot to mention—we're getting a few new residents at mid-week. We'll be full up in all ten cells. So we're checking the surveillance equipment in the empty cells to make sure everything's working right. We've also increased the security staff on each shift from four officers to six during the day, not including me, and from three to four at night."

"That's sounds…risky," Jessie said diplomatically.

"I fought it," Kat admitted. "But the county had a need and we had available cells. It was a losing battle."

Jessie nodded as she looked around. The fundamentals of the place seemed the same. The unit was designed like a wheel with a command center in the middle and spokes extending out in every direction, leading to inmate cells. There were currently six officers in the now-cramped space of the command center, which looked like an extremely busy hospital nurses' station.

A few of the faces were new to her but most were familiar, including Ernie Cortez. Ernie was a massive specimen of a man, about six foot six and 250 well-muscled pounds. He was in his thirties and just starting to show bits of gray in his close-cropped black hair. He gave a big grin when he saw Jessie.

"Vogue chick," he called out, using the affectionate nickname he'd given her on their first meeting when she'd shown up and he tried to hit on her, suggesting she should be a model. She'd shut him down pretty fast but he didn't seem to hold a grudge.

"How's it going, Ernie?" she asked, smiling back.

"You know; same old. Making sure pedophiles, rapists, and murderers mind their P's and Q's. You?"

"Mostly the same," she said, deciding not to get into the particulars of her activities the last few months with so many unfamiliar faces around.

"So now that you've had a few months to get over your divorce, you want to spend a little quality time with the Ernster? I'm planning to go to Tijuana this weekend."

"The Ernster?" Jessie repeated, unable to stop herself from giggling.

"What?" he said, faux-defensively. "It's a nickname."

"I'm sorry, Ernster, but I'm pretty sure I'm going to have plans this weekend. But you have fun at the jai alai track. Buy some Chiclets for me, okay?"

"Ouch," he replied, grabbing at his chest as if she'd shot an arrow in his heart. "You know, big boys have feelings too. We're also, you know ... big boys."

"All right, Cortez," Kat interjected, "enough of that. You just made me throw up a little in my mouth. And Jessie has business to attend to."

"Hurtful," Ernie muttered under his breath as he returned his attention to the monitor in front of him, Despite his words, his tone suggested he wasn't all that broken up. Kat motioned for Jessie to follow her to the spoke with Crutchfield's cell.

"You'll want this," she said, holding up the small key fob with the red button in the middle. It was the "in case of emergency, break glass" device. Jessie considered it a kind of digital security blanket.

If Crutchfield was messing with her head and she wanted to leave the room without letting him know the impact he was having, she was to push the button hidden in her hand. That would alert Kat, who could remove her from the room for some official, made-up reason. Jessie was pretty sure Crutchfield was aware of the device but she was glad to have it nonetheless.

She grabbed the key fob, nodded to Kat that she was ready to enter, and took a deep breath. Kat opened the door and Jessie stepped inside.

Apparently Crutchfield had anticipated her arrival. He was standing up, only inches from the glass wall dividing the room in half, smiling broadly at her.

CHAPTER SIX

It took Jessie a second to rip her eyes away from his crooked teeth and evaluate the situation.

On the surface, he didn't look that different than she remembered. He still had the blond hair, shorn close to his head. He still wore the same mandatory aqua-blue scrubs. He still had the slightly pudgier face than one would expect of a man who was about five foot eight and 150 pounds. It made him look closer to twenty-five than the thirty-five years old he was.

And he still had the probing, almost stalking brown eyes. They were the only hint that the man across from her had killed at nineteen least people and perhaps twice that many.

The cell hadn't changed either. It was small, with a narrow sheetless bed bolted to the far wall. A small desk with an attached chair sat in the back right corner beside a small metal wash basin. Behind that was a toilet, set off in the back, with a sliding plastic door for a modicum of privacy.

"Miss Jessie," he purred softly. "What an unexpected surprise running into you here."

"And yet, you're standing there as if you expected my imminent arrival," Jessie countered, not wanting to give Crutchfield even a moment's advantage. She walked over and sat down in the chair behind a small desk on the other side of the glass. Kat took up her usual position, standing alertly in the corner of the room.

"I sensed a change in the energy of this facility," he replied, his Louisiana accent as pronounced as ever. "The air seemed sweeter and I thought I could hear a bird chirping outside."

"You're not usually this full of flattery," Jessie noted. "Care to share what has you in such a complimentary mood?"

"Nothing in particular, Miss Jessie. Can't a man just appreciate the small joy that comes from having an unexpected visitor?"

Something in the way he said that last line made Jessie's scalp tingle, as if there was more to the comment. She sat quietly for a moment, allowing her mind to work, unconcerned about any time constraints. She knew Kat would let her handle the interview however she chose.

Turning over Crutchfield's words in her head, she realized they might have more than one meaning.

"When you talk about unexpected visitors, are you referring to me, Mr. Crutchfield?"

He stared at her for several seconds without speaking. Finally, slowly, the wide, forced smile on his face twisted into a more malevolent—and more believable—smirk.

"We haven't established the ground rules for this visit," he said, suddenly turning his back on her.

"I think the days of ground rules have long since passed, don't you, Mr. Crutchfield?" she asked. "We've known each other long enough that we can just talk, can't we?"

He walked back to the bed attached to the back wall of the cell and sat down, his expression slightly hidden in shadow now.

"But how can I be certain that you'll be as forthcoming as you'd like me to be with you?" he asked.

"After ordering one of your flunkies to break into my friend's apartment and scaring her to the point that she still can't sleep, I'm not sure you've fully earned my trust or my willingness to be accommodating."

"You bring up that incident," he said, "but you neglect to mention the multiple times I've assisted you in cases both professional and personal. For every so-called indiscretion on my part, I've compensated with information that has proved invaluable to you. All I'm asking for are assurances that this won't be a one-way street."

Jessie looked at him hard, trying to determine how accommodating she could be while still keeping a professional distance.

"What is it exactly that you're looking for?"

"Right now? Just your time, Miss Jessie. I'd prefer you not be such a stranger. It's been seventy-six days since you last graced me with your presence. A less confident man than myself might take offense at the long absence."

"Okay," Jessie said. "I promise to visit you on a more regular basis. In fact, I'll make sure to stop by at least once more this week. How does that sound?"

"It's a start," he replied noncommittally.

"Great. Then let's get back to my question. You said before that you appreciated the joy that comes from having an unexpected visitor. Were you referring to me?"

"Miss Jessie, while it is always a delight to revel in your company, I must confess that my comment was indeed in reference to another visitor."

Jessie could sense Kat stiffen in the corner behind her.

"And who are you referring to?" she asked, keeping her voice level.

"I think you know."

I'd like you to tell me," Jessie insisted.

Bolton Crutchfield stood up again, now more visible in the full light, and Jessie could see that he was rolling his tongue around in his mouth, like it was a fish on a line that he was toying with.

"As I assured you the last time that we spoke, I would be having a chat with your daddy."

"And have you?"

"I have indeed," he answered as casually as if he were telling her the time. "He asked me to pass along his regards, after I offered yours."

Jessie stared at him closely, looking for any hint of deception in his face.

"You spoke to Xander Thurman," she reconfirmed, "in this room, sometime in the last eleven weeks?"

"I did."

Jessie knew that Kat was bursting to ask her own questions in order to try to confirm the veracity of his claim and how it might have happened. But in her mind, that was secondary and could be addressed later. She didn't want the conversation to get sidetracked so she followed up before her friend could say anything.

"What did you discuss?' she asked, trying to keep the judgment out of her voice.

"Well, we had to be rather cryptic, so as not to reveal his true identity to those listening in. But the gist of our chat was about you, Miss Jessie."

"Me?"

"Yes. If you'll recall, he and I chatted a couple of years ago and he warned me that you might one day visit. But that you would have a different name than the one he'd given you, Jessica Thurman."

Jessie flinched involuntarily at the name she hadn't heard spoken aloud by anyone but herself in two decades. She knew he saw her reaction but there was nothing she could do about it. Crutchfield smiled knowingly and continued.

"He wanted to know how his long-lost daughter was doing. He was interested in all kinds of details—what you do for a living, where you live, what you look like now, what your new name is. He's very anxious to reconnect, Miss Jessie."

As he spoke, Jessie told herself to breathe slowly in and out. She reminded herself to unclench her body and do her best to look calm, even if it was a facade. She had to appear unperturbed as she asked her next question.

"Did you share any of those details with him?"

"Just one," he said impishly.

"And what was that?"

"Home is where the heart is," he said.

"What the hell does that mean?" she demanded, her heart suddenly beating rapidly.

"I told him the location of the place you call home," he said matter-of-factly.

"You gave him my address?"

"I wasn't that specific. To be honest, I don't know your exact address, despite my best efforts to uncover it. But I know enough for him find his way to you if he's smart. And as we both know, Miss Jessie, your daddy is very smart."

Jessie gulped hard and fought the urge to scream at him. He was still answering her questions and she needed as much information as she could get before he stopped.

"So how long do I have before he knocks on my door?"

"That depends on how long it takes for him to put the pieces together," Crutchfield said with an exaggerated shrug. "As I said, I had to be a bit cryptic. If I had been too specific, it would have sent off warning signs with the folks who monitor my every conversation. That wouldn't have been productive."

"Why don't you tell me exactly what you told him? That way, I can figure out the likely timetable for myself."

"Now where's the fun in that, Miss Jessie? I'm quite taken with you. But that strikes me as an unreasonable advantage. We have to give the man a chance."

"A chance?" Jessie repeated, disbelieving. "To what? Get a head start on gutting me like he did my mother?"

"Now that hardly seems fair," he replied, seeming to get calmer the more agitated Jessie became. "He could have done that back in that snowy cabin all those years ago. But he didn't. So why assume he means you harm now? Maybe he just wants to take his little lady to Disneyland for the day."

"You'll forgive me if I'm not as inclined to give him the benefit of the doubt," she spat. "This isn't a game, Bolton. You want me to visit you again? I need to be alive to do that. I won't be very chatty if your mentor chops up your favorite gal pal."

"Two things, Miss Jessie: first of all, I understand that this is disruptive news, but I'd prefer you not take such a familiar tone with me. Calling me by my first name? That's not only unprofessional, it's unbecoming of you."

Jessie seethed silently. Even before he told her the second thing, she knew he wasn't going to tell her what she wanted. Still, she remained silent, literally biting her tongue in case he had a change of heart.

"And second," he continued, clearly enjoying watching her squirm, "while I do enjoy your company, don't presume that you're my favorite gal pal. Let's not forget about the ever-vigilant Officer Gentry there behind you. She's a real peach—a rotting, rancid peach. As I've told her on more than one occasion, when I depart this place, I intend to give her a special send-off, if you take my meaning. So please don't try to jump the gal pal line."

"I…" Jessie began, hoping to change his mind.

"Our time is up, I'm afraid," he said curtly. With that, he turned and walked over to the tiny niche of the cell with the toilet in it and pulled the plastic divider across, ending the conversation.

CHAPTER SEVEN

Jessie kept her head on a swivel, on the lookout for anyone or anything out of the ordinary.

As she returned to her place, following the same circuitous route as earlier in the day, all the security precautions she'd been so proud of only hours earlier now seemed woefully inadequate.

This time around, she tied her hair into a bun and hid it under a baseball cap and the hood of a sweatshirt she bought on the way back from Norwalk. Her small backpack purse was attached in the front so that it hugged her chest. Despite the added anonymity they might have provided, she didn't wear sunglasses out of concern they would limit her line of sight.

Kat had promised to review the tape of all Crutchfield's recent visits to see if they'd missed something. She also said that if Jessie could wait until work ended, she'd make the drive to DTLA, even though she lived in far-off City of Industry, and help ensure that she got back safe. Jessie politely declined the offer.

"I can't count on having an armed escort everywhere I go from now on," she'd insisted.

"Why not?" Kat had asked only half-jokingly.

Now, as she walked down the corridor to her apartment, she wondered if she should have taken her friend up on the offer. She felt especially vulnerable with the bag of groceries in her arms. The hall was deathly quiet and she hadn't seen anyone at all since entering the building. Before she could dismiss it out of hand, a crazy notion popped into her head—that her father had killed everyone on her floor so that he wouldn't have to deal with complications when he approached her.

Her peephole light was green, which gave her some assurance as she opened the door, looking down both ends of the hall for anyone who might jump out at her. No one did. Once inside, she flicked on the lights and then turned all the locks back before disarming both alarms. Immediately after, she rearmed the main one in "home" mode so that she could move about the apartment without setting off the motions sensors.

She put the grocery bag on the kitchen counter and searched the place, nightstick in hand. She had successfully applied for a firearms permit before she left for Quantico and was supposed to get her weapon when she went to the station for work tomorrow. Part of her wished she had just picked it up when she stopped by to get her mail earlier today. When she was finally confident that the apartment was secure, she began to put the groceries away, leaving out the sashimi she'd picked up for dinner instead of pizza.

Nothing like supermarket sushi on Monday night to make a single gal feel special in the big city.

The thought made her chuckle to herself briefly before she remembered that her serial killer father had been given a guide to her place of residence. Maybe it wasn't a complete roadmap. But from what Crutchfield had said, it was enough for him to eventually find her. The big question was: when was "eventually"?

Ninety minutes later, Jessie was punching a heavy bag, sweat pouring off her body. After finishing her sushi, she had felt restless and cooped up and decided to work out her frustrations in a constructive way at the gym.

She'd never been much of a workout fiend. But while at the National Academy she'd come to an unexpected discovery. When she worked out to exhaustion, there was no space left inside her for the anxiety and fear that consumed her so much of the rest of the time. If only she'd known this a decade ago, she could have saved herself thousands of sleepless nights, even the nights filled with endless nightmares.

It might also have saved her a few trips to see her therapist, Dr. Janice Lemmon, a renowned forensic psychologist in her own right. Dr. Lemmon was one of the few people who knew every detail about Jessie's past. She'd been an invaluable resource in recent years.

But she was currently in recovery from a kidney transplant and wasn't available for sessions for a few more weeks. Jessie was tempted to think she could dispense with the visits altogether. But while it might be cheaper to go with workout therapy alone, she knew there would surely be times she'd need to see the doctor in the future.

As she went in for a series of jabs, she recalled how, prior to her trip to Quantico, she'd often wake up covered in perspiration, breathing heavily, trying to remind herself that she was safe in Los Angeles and not back in a small cabin in the Missouri Ozarks, tied to a chair, watching blood drip from the slowly freezing body of her dead mother.

If only that had just been a dream too. But it was all real. When she was six years old and her parents' marriage was on the rocks, her father had taken her and her mother to his remote cabin. While there, he revealed that he'd been abducting, torturing, and killing people for years. And then he did the same to his own wife, Carrie Thurman.

As he manacled her hands to the ceiling beams of the cabin and intermittently stabbed her with a knife, he made Jessie—then Jessica Thurman—watch. He tied her arms to a chair and taped her eyelids open as he finally cut her mother open for good.

Then he used the same knife to slice a large gash across his own daughter's collarbone from her left shoulder to the base of her neck. After that, he simply left the cabin. It was three days later when, hypothermic and in shock, she was discovered by two hunters who had just happened by.

After she recovered, she told the police and FBI the story. But by then, her dad was long gone and any hope of catching him was gone with it. Jessica was put into Witness Protection in Las Cruces with the Hunts. Jessica Thurman became Jessie Hunt and a new life began.

Jessie shook the memories out of her head, switching from jabs to knee kicks intended for an attacker's groin. She embraced the ache in her quad as she slammed it upward. With each blow, the image of her mother's pale, lifeless skin faded.

Then another memory popped into her head, that of her former husband, Kyle, attacking her in their own home, trying to kill her and frame her for the murder of his mistress. She could almost feel the sting of the fireplace poker he jammed into the left side of her abdomen.

The physical pain of that moment was only matched by the humiliation she still felt at having spent a decade involved with a sociopath and never realizing it. She was, after all, supposed to be an expert at identifying these kinds of people.

Jessie switched it up again, hoping to push the shame out of her mind with a series of elbow shots to the bag near where an assailant's jaw would be. Her shoulders were starting to shout at her in displeasure but she continued pummeling the bag, knowing that her mind would soon be too tired to be distressed.

This was the part of herself she hadn't expected to discover at the FBI—the physical badass. Despite the standard apprehension she felt when she arrived, she had suspected she'd do well on the academic side of things. She had just spent the previous three years in that environment, immersed in criminal psychology.

And she'd been right. The classes in law, forensic science, and terrorism had come easy. Even the behavior science seminar, where the instructors were heroes of hers and she thought she'd be nervous, came naturally. But it had been the physical fitness classes, and the self-defense training in particular, where she'd surprised herself the most.

Her instructors had shown her that at five-foot-ten and 145 pounds, she had the physical size to contend with most perpetrators if she was properly prepared. She would likely never have the hand-to-hand combat skills of a former Special Forces veteran like Kat Gentry. But she left the program confident that she could defend herself in most situations.

Jessie yanked off the gloves and moved to the treadmill. Glancing at the clock, she saw that it was approaching 8 p.m. She decided that a solid five-mile run should wipe her out enough to let her sleep dream-free tonight. That was a priority as she started back at work tomorrow where she knew all her colleagues would give her crap, expecting her to be some kind of FBI superhero now.

She set the time for forty minutes, putting pressure on herself to complete the five miles at an eight-minute-per-mile pace. Then she turned up the volume on her ear buds. As the first few seconds of Seal's "Killer" started to play, her mind went blank, focusing only on the task in front of her. She was completely oblivious to the song's title or any personal memories it might conjure up. There was only the beat and her legs pounding in harmony with it. It was as close to peace as Jessie Hunt could get.

CHAPTER EIGHT

Eliza Longworth hurried to Penny's front door as quickly as she could. It was almost 8 a.m., which was when their yoga instructor usually showed up.

It had been a largely sleepless night. Only in the first light of morning did she feel like she knew the path she had to take. Once the decision was made, Eliza felt a weight lift off her.

She texted Penny to tell her that the long night had given her time to think, and to reconsider if she'd been too hasty in ending their friendship. They should do the yoga lesson. And then afterward, once their instructor, Beth, had gone, they could try to find a way to hash things out.

Penny hadn't replied but that didn't stop Eliza from going over anyway. Just as she reached the front door, she saw Beth driving up the winding residential road and waved to her.

"Penny!" she yelled as she knocked on the door. "Beth's here. Are we still on for yoga?"

There was no answer so she pushed the Ring doorbell and waved her arms in front of the camera.

"Penny, can I come in? We should talk for a sec before Beth arrives."

There was still no answer and Beth was only about a hundred yards down the road so she decided to go in. She knew where the secret key was kept but tried the door anyway. It was unlocked. She stepped inside, leaving the door open for Beth.

"Penny," she called out. "You left the door unlocked. Beth's pulling up. Did you get my text? Can we talk privately for a minute before we start?"

She walked into the foyer and waited. There was still no response. She moved into the living room where they usually had the yoga sessions. It was empty too. She was about to go to the kitchen when Beth walked in.

"Ladies, I'm here!" she called out from the front door.

"Hey, Beth," Eliza said, turning to greet her. "The door was unlocked but Penny's not answering. I'm not sure what's up. Maybe she overslept or is in the bathroom or something. I can check upstairs if you want to get yourself something to drink. I'm sure it'll just be a minute."

"No problem," Beth said. "My nine thirty client cancelled so I'm not in a hurry. Tell her to take her time."

"Okay," Eliza said as she started up the stairs. "Just give us a minute."

She was about halfway up the first flight of stairs when she wondered if perhaps she should have taken the elevator. The master bedroom was on the third floor and she wasn't enthused about the hike. Before she could seriously reconsider, she heard a scream from down below.

"What is it?" she yelled as she turned and rushed back down.

"Hurry!" Beth shouted. "Dear god, hurry!"

Her voice was coming from the kitchen. Eliza broke into a run once she got to the bottom of the stairs, tearing through the living room and rounding the corner.

On the Spanish tile kitchen floor, lying in a massive pool of blood, was Penny. Her eyes were frozen open in terror, her body contorted into some horrifying death spasm.

Eliza hurried over to her oldest, dearest friend, slipping on the thick liquid as she approached. Her foot slid out from under her and she landed hard on the ground, her whole body splashing in the blood.

Trying not to gag, she crawled over and put her hands on Penny's chest. Even with clothes on, she was cold. Despite that, Eliza shook her, as if that might wake her up.

"Penny," she begged, "wake up."

Her friend didn't respond. Eliza looked up at Beth.

"Do you know CPR?' she asked.

"No," the younger woman said in a quavering voice, shaking her head. "But I think it's too late."

Ignoring the comment, Eliza tried to remember the CPR class she'd taken years ago. It was for treating children but the same principles should apply. She opened Penny's mouth, tilted her head back, pinched her nose, and blew hard down her friend's throat.

Then she climbed on top of Penny's waist, put one hand on top of the other with her palms down, and thrust the pad of her hand down into Penny's sternum. She did it a second time and then a third, trying to get into some kind of rhythm.

"Oh god," she heard Beth mutter and looked up to see what was going on.

"What is it?" she demanded harshly.

"When you push on her, blood oozes out of her chest."

Eliza looked down. It was true. Each compression caused a slow leak of blood from what appeared to be wide gashes in her chest cavity. She looked up again.

"Call nine-one-one!" she screamed, though she knew there was no point.

Jessie, who felt unexpectedly nervous, got to work early.

With all of the extra security precautions she had in place, she'd decided to leave for her first day of work in three months twenty minutes early to make sure she arrived by 9 a.m., the time Captain Decker had told her to show up. But she must have been getting better at negotiating all the hidden turns and stairwells because it didn't take nearly as long as she expected to get to Central Station.

As she walked from the parking structure to the main entrance of the station, her eyes darted back and forth, looking for anything out of the ordinary. But then she remembered the promise she'd made to herself just before she fell asleep last night. She would not allow the threat from her father to consume her.

She had no idea how vague or specific Bolton Crutchfield's information to her father had been. She couldn't even be sure that Crutchfield was telling her the truth. Regardless, there wasn't much more she could do about it than she was already doing. Kat Gentry was checking the tapes of Crutchfield's visits. She basically lived in a bunker. She'd be getting her official weapon today. Beyond that, she had to live her life. Otherwise she'd go crazy.

She made her way back to the station's main bullpen, more than a little apprehensive at the reception she'd receive after so long away. Add to that, when she'd last been here she was merely an interim junior profiling consultant.

Now the interim tag was gone and, though she was technically still a consultant, she was paid by the LAPD and got all the attendant benefits. That included health insurance, which if recent experience was any example, she'd need in spades.

When she stepped into the large central work area, comprised of dozens of desks, separated by nothing more than corkboards, she breathed in and waited. But there was nothing. No one said anything.

In fact, no one even seemed to notice her arrival. Some heads were down, studying case files. Others were fixed on the people across the tables from them, in most cases witnesses or handcuffed suspects.

She felt slightly deflated. But more than that, she felt silly.

What did I expect—a parade?

It's not like she won the mythical Nobel Prize for crime solving. She'd gone to an FBI training academy for two and a half months. It was pretty cool. But no one was going to break out in applause for her.

She walked quietly through the maze of desks, passing detectives she'd worked with previously. Callum Reid, in his mid-forties, glanced up from the file he was reading. As he nodded at her, his glasses almost fell off his forehead, where they had been resting.

Twenty-something Alan Trembley, his blond curls messy as usual, was wearing glasses too, but his were at the bridge of his nose as he intently questioned an older man who appeared to be drunk. He didn't even notice Jessie as she walked past him.

She reached her desk, which was embarrassingly tidy, tossed down her jacket and backpack purse, and took a seat. As she did, she saw Garland Moses slowly amble from the break room, coffee in hand, as he started up the stairs to his second-floor office in what was essentially a broom closet.

It seemed a rather unimpressive workspace for the most celebrated criminal profiler the LAPD had but Moses didn't appear to care. In fact, he couldn't be bothered about much. Over seventy years old and working as a consultant for the department mostly to avoid boredom, the legendary profiler could do pretty much whatever he wanted. A former FBI agent, he'd moved to the West Coast to retire but had been convinced to consult for the department. He agreed, as long as he could pick his cases and work his hours. Considering his track record, no one objected at the time and they still didn't now.

With a shock of unkempt white hair, leathery skin, and a wardrobe circa 1981, he had a reputation of being crusty at best and downright surly at worst. But in Jessie's one significant interaction with him, she'd found him to be, if not warm, at least conversational. She wanted to pick his brain more but was still a bit frightened to engage him directly.

As he shuffled up the stairs and out of sight, she glanced around, looking for Ryan Hernandez, the detective she'd worked with most often and whom she felt borderline comfortable calling her friend. They'd even recently started using each other's first name, a huge deal in cop circles.

They had actually met under non-professional circumstances, when her professor invited him to speak to her graduate criminal psychology class in her final semester at UC-Irvine last fall. He'd presented a case study, which Jessie, alone in the class, had been able to solve. Later, she learned she was only the second person ever to figure it out.

After that, they'd stayed in touch. She'd call him for help after she began to grow suspicious of her husband's motives but before he tried to kill her. And once she'd moved back to DTLA, she was assigned to Central Station, where he was based.

They worked several cases together, including the murder of high society philanthropist Victoria Missinger. It was in large part Jessie's discovery of the killer that had garnered the respect that secured her the FBI gig. And it wouldn't have been possible without Ryan Hernandez's experience and instincts.

In fact, he was so well regarded that he'd been assigned to a special unit in Robbery-Homicide called Homicide Special Section, or HSS for short. They specialized in high-profile cases that engendered lots of media interest or public scrutiny. That usually meant arsons, murders with multiple victims, murders of notable individuals, and, of course, serial killers.

Beyond his gifts as an investigator, Jessie had to acknowledge that he wasn't unpleasant to spend time with. The two of them had an easy rapport, as if they'd known each other much longer than six months. On a few occasions at Quantico, when her guard was down, Jessie wondered if things might have been different if they'd met under other circumstances. But at the time, Jessie had still been married and Hernandez and his wife had been together for over six years.

Just then Captain Roy Decker opened his office door and stepped out. Tall, skinny, and almost completely bald save for a few stray hairs, Decker was not yet sixty. But he looked much older than that, with a sallow, lined face that suggested constant stress. His nose came to a sharp point and his small eyes were alert, as if always on the hunt, which Jessie supposed he was.

As he stepped into the bullpen, someone followed him out. It was Ryan. He was just as she'd remembered him. About six feet tall and two hundred pounds with short black hair and brown eyes, he wore a coat and tie that hid what she knew to be a well-muscled frame.

He was thirty years old, young to be a full detective. But he had moved up fast, especially after, as a street officer, he'd helped catch a notorious serial killer named Bolton Crutchfield.

As he and Captain Decker walked out, something his boss said made him break into that warm, easy grin that was so disarming, even to suspects he was questioning. Much to her surprise, the sight of it caused an unexpected reaction in her. Somewhere in her stomach, she got a strange sensation she hadn't felt in years: butterflies.

Hernandez caught sight of her and waved as the two men walked over. She stood up, annoyed at the unexpected feeling and hoping movement would stifle it. Forcing her brain into professional mode, she tried to discern what they might have been talking about privately based on their expressions. But both men wore masks that suggested they were trying to keep the content of their discussion private. Jessie did notice one thing, however: Ryan looked tired.

"Welcome back, Hunt," Decker said perfunctorily. "I trust your time in Virginia was illuminating?"

"Very much so, sir," she replied.

"Excellent. While I would love to hear about the particulars, we'll have to hold off on that for now, Instead, you're going to put your new skills to the test right away. You've got a case."

"Sir?" she said, slightly surprised. She assumed he'd want to ease her back in and go over her new duties as a full-time non-interim profiler.

"Hernandez will explain the details to you en route," Decker said. "The case is a bit sensitive and your services were specifically requested."

"Really?" Jessie asked, regretting her enthusiasm the moment she said it.

"Really, Hunt," Decker answered, scowling slightly. "Apparently you've developed a bit of a reputation as the Suburbia Whisperer. I can't go into any more now. Suffice to say, the folks upstairs want this case handled delicately. I expect you'll keep that in mind as you proceed."

"Yes sir."

"All right. We'll catch up later," he said. Then he turned and walked off without another word.

Ryan, who hadn't spoken until then, finally did now.

"Welcome home," he said. "How are you doing?"

"Not too bad," she said, ignoring the fluttering sensation that had suddenly returned. "Just getting back into the flow of things, you know?"

"Well, diving right back in should help," he said. "We've got to head out right away."

"Do I have time to pick up the weapon I requisitioned before I left for Quantico?"

"I checked on that for you earlier this morning," he said as they began walking through the bullpen. "Unfortunately, there was some kind of bureaucratic screw-up and it hadn't been processed yet. I resolved the paperwork issue but you probably won't get your gun until next week. Think you can survive just using your brain as a weapon for a few days?"

He smiled at her but she noticed something she hadn't picked up on earlier. He had shadows under his eyes, which were a little red.

"Sure," she said, nodding, trying to keep up with his brisk pace. "Is everything okay?"

"Yeah. Why?" he asked, glancing over at her.

"You just look a little ... tired."

"Yeah," he said, looking straight ahead again as he talked. "I've had a bit of trouble sleeping lately. Shelly and I are getting separated."

CHAPTER NINE

They had been in the car for several minutes before things felt normal again.

Jessie had offered her sympathies back at the station and Ryan had thanked her. But he hadn't been forthcoming beyond that and she didn't think that asking any questions was appropriate. And since whatever case they were handling was too sensitive to discuss inside the station, they were reduced to awkward chitchat about her flight back and the perils of supermarket sushi. They were out of rhythm.

At first, things were no better once they got on the road. As they pulled onto the street from the garage, a homeless guy knocked on her window asking for spare change. She jumped in her seat, hitting her head on the roof.

"You okay?" Ryan asked, giving her a sideways glance.

"Yeah, I guess I'm just out of practice," she said as she rubbed the sore spot. "There aren't as many homeless guys on the streets of suburban Virginia."

Ryan looked like he was about to respond, then thought better of it. Things got a bit better once they started moving through traffic.

"So what's so sensitive about this case that we couldn't discuss it at the station?" she asked.

"We probably could have," Ryan admitted, as he pulled onto the freeway heading west. "But Decker can be a bit paranoid and I find it's easier to roll with it than to fight it. We're going to Pacific Palisades."

"That's a little out of our area, isn't it?"

Yeah, by about twenty miles. But even though it's almost to Malibu, it's technically part of the city of Los Angeles, so it's in LAPD jurisdiction. The folks at the West LA station caught a case they thought we could help with. Actually, they thought *you* could help. I'm just along for the ride."

"Wait, what?" Jessie asked, completely confused.

"Let me back up a little bit," Ryan said. "Sometime in the last twelve hours, a woman named Penelope Wooten was murdered. She was stabbed at least eight times in the chest and abdomen. My old partner, Brady Bowen, caught the case. It turns out that Penelope is married to Colton Wooten. Does that name ring a bell?"

"No. Should it?"

"Maybe not yet," Ryan said. "But his profile was about to get much higher. Wooten is a former assistant district attorney who now runs a mega practice in Santa Monica. But word is he was on the verge of declaring his candidacy for DA in a few months. And most folks thought he had a solid chance to win."

"Is that why Decker said this has to be handled delicately?"

"That's a big part of it. Obviously when a wife is killed in what looks like a crime of passion, the husband is automatically a prime suspect. So we're already in an inherently sensitive situation before we even start investigating."

"I don't know that I'm especially qualified to navigate something like that," Jessie admitted.

"No," Ryan agreed. "In fact, you're probably less so than most."

"Thanks for that," she said, smirking.

"Sorry. But it's true. Having said that, what you *are* qualified for is dealing with crimes involving wealthy people in exclusive neighborhoods. And the residents of hillside ocean-view estates in Pacific Palisades definitely go in that bucket."

"I've solved one case, Ryan," she said skeptically.

"Officially," he countered. "But unofficially, you also solved the case involving your husband. And your life leading up to that was immersed in that world—mansions, country clubs, people who burn their own cash for fun."

"That might be overstating it just a bit," she said, trying not to laugh.

"You get my point," he pressed. "You lived among these kinds of people. You *were* one of these people. You get them. You understand how they think. That's a valuable gift."

"Thanks, I guess," Jessie said, uncomfortable with the compliment. "But how did folks all the way out in Pacific Palisades hear about some junior profiler in the downtown area?"

"World travels in law enforcement," he answered. "Also, I may have had a drink with Brady a few weeks ago and mentioned you in passing."

"Okay," Jessie said, not sure how else to respond.

"Anyway," Ryan said, barreling past that exchange as quickly as possible, "when this case came up, he thought of you. And having worked with him, it just made sense for me to tag along. His most recent partner just retired so I'll team up with him for the case and you'll be the assigned profiler. Sound good?"

"Sounds like I don't have much choice," Jessie said.

"Are you bummed about having to investigate a case with ocean views and an elevator in the house?"

"I just...it's true that I know this world. But my memories of it aren't great. And if the folks who live here are anything like the ones I knew in Westport Beach, we're going to be dealing with some real prima donnas. That doesn't excite me."

"Well, I've got good and bad news."

"Bad news first," Jessie insisted. "Always give me the bad news first."

"The bad news is, from my experience, you are indeed entering prima donna territory."

"So what's the good news?"

"I know a great seafood place we can go for lunch."

"We're headed to a murder scene and you're thinking about lunch spots?" Jessie asked incredulously.

"Always," Ryan replied with an almost disturbing level of enthusiasm.

❧ ❧ ❧

The Wooten house rested inside what could only be called a compound.

They had to enter through a gate at the bottom of the hill, which was manned by an officer checking identification. The drive up to the house was an almost quarter-mile-long stretch of hairpin turns. There was a second gate along a wall surrounding the house, which also had an officer standing guard.

"Both gates have code panels," Ryan noted as they passed through. "That would make it hard for too many outsiders to get in."

"Yep," Jessie agreed. "And you wouldn't even know there was a house up here from the road. Also, without having seen the body, getting stabbed eight times doesn't sound like the work of some random home invasion robbery gone wrong. It feels personal."

Detective Brady Bowen was waiting for them when they pulled up into the massive circular driveway. He wasn't what Jessie had imagined a detective from a fancy coastal community would look like. Squat, with a barrel chest, an ample gut, a mustache, sweat pouring off his brow and shirttails poking out of his slacks, which looked about to burst at the seams, he reminded her of Andy Sipowicz, her adoptive father's favorite character from that 1990s show *NYPD Blue.*

When they stepped out of the car, he gave Ryan a big bear hug and then turned to Jessie. Up close, she noticed that his bright blue eyes sparkled with warmth and enthusiasm.

"Great to meet you, Ms. Hunt. I hear super things," he said, wiping his hand on his pants and politely shaking hers.

"Nice you meet you too. And please call me Jessie."

"Only if you call me the Bradenator," he said, before adding, "Just kidding, Brady works fine."

"Hey, Bradenator," Ryan said with not a little sarcasm. "What have we got here?"

"Always straight to business with this guy," Brady said, winking at Jessie. "Okay, here's the situation. Penelope Wooten, age thirty-four. Married seven years to Colton Wooten. Two children—Colt Jr., age six, and Anastasia, four. She was found around eight a.m. this morning by her yoga teacher, Beth Copeland, and neighbor and best friend, Eliza Longworth. They had a session scheduled for today. There were eight deep stab wounds in her chest and abdomen, along with a few smaller defensive ones on her hands. It looks like she may have fallen while trying to fend off the attack, then gotten the worst of it when she was on the ground."

"Time of death?" Ryan asked.

"It's too early for anything definitive yet but we're likely looking at some time between midnight and seven a.m. No sign of forced entry. The best friend says the front door was unlocked."

"Are the friend and yoga teacher inside now?" Jessie asked.

"The yoga teacher, Copeland, is out back," Brady told her. "The friend, Longworth, had to go to the hospital. When she saw the victim, she ran over to give her CPR and slipped in the blood. She landed pretty hard and bruised up her knee. She was also covered in blood from trying to administer CPR. When the paramedics arrived she was pretty freaked out and they recommended she go to the hospital. It looked like she might be in shock. An officer went with her to take her statement."

"Are we certain she got all the blood on her from slipping in it?" Jessie asked skeptically.

"That was my first thought too," Brady said. "But the yoga teacher said she didn't have a drop on her until she fell. She was right there when it happened."

"Is Mr. Wooten here yet?" Ryan asked with trepidation.

"Ah yes," Brady said in an unenthusiastic tone. "The counselor is in the dining room right now. Believe me—I wouldn't be making Bradenator jokes if he was in hearing range. An officer asked some preliminary questions, but I haven't spoken to him yet. I figured I'd wait so we could all get his answers for the first time together."

"Did the officer have any initial thoughts?" Jessie asked.

"He described Wooten as distraught and confrontational. Not surprising but not much fun either."

"Well, I guess we should check out the body," Ryan said. "Then we can talk to Beth Copeland while things are still fresh for her. Is Wooten going to balk if he has to wait?"

"I think we can hold him off a bit," Brady assured him. "The officer can tell him that we'll meet with him once we've done our due diligence—crime scene investigation, witness interviews, et cetera. He's an officer of the court. Even under these circumstances, he should understand."

"I also think we should talk to Eliza Longworth as soon as possible," Jessie added, "preferably before she gets too cleaned up. I want her raw answers, before she's had too much time to regroup."

"Not a problem," Brady said. "She was only taken away about twenty minutes ago. I'll give instructions for her not to change or shower until we've spoken to her. Shall we go in?"

Jessie and Ryan nodded and followed Brady toward the house. As they approached, Jessie craned her neck to take the whole place in. It was a three-story, Spanish-style mansion built into the side of a hill overlooking the Pacific Ocean, which glimmered about a half mile off in the distance. Other similarly situated homes dotted this hill and others nearby. They were all impressive but from what Jessie could see, most of them weren't gated.

They stepped into the foyer. Almost immediately she noted that next to the base of the stairs was an elevator. She had thought Ryan was joking. Brady led them through the expansive living room into the kitchen, handing them each latex gloves before they entered. As Jessie put them on, she steeled herself, aware that once she rounded the corner, she would be looking at something awful.

It was worse than she'd expected. The other high-profile woman whose murder she had solved, a Hancock Park philanthropist named Victoria Missinger, had been poisoned. There was no overt sign of violence and she had looked like she was sleeping. That was not the case here.

Penelope Wooten lay face-up on the Spanish kitchen tile, surrounded by a large, now-congealing puddle of blood that had matted her long blonde hair. She was wearing a yoga outfit, which was punctured at various points on her torso by multiple knife wounds.

But that wasn't what got to Jessie. She'd seen knife wounds and dead bodies up close before. It was the woman's eyes. They were wide open, fixed with the twin emotions she must have felt at the time of her death: fear and confusion. They seemed to be simultaneously pleading for help and asking why.

Jessie knew she couldn't do anything about the first request. But she silently swore to answer the second part—why had this happened and not just that: who did it?

CHAPTER TEN

The more Jessie studied the crime scene, the more certain she was that Penelope had known the killer.

As she walked around the kitchen, she tried to employ the tactics she'd just learned in her behavioral science seminars at the FBI training academy. Her instructors had preached one overriding principle: let the evidence guide your conclusions.

It seemed like logical advice but it required a mindset change for Jessie. She had always let her instincts be her guide. She seemed to have a gift for reading people, at least people she didn't know. But she'd come to realize she'd gotten too dependent on that skill.

On more than one occasion, she'd ignored evidence that could have helped her solve a case because her gut was sending her down a different path. She realized she was especially susceptible to giving those she liked the benefit of the doubt. That was partly why she hadn't picked up on the clues that her ex-husband was a sociopath. It was also why she was almost killed by Victoria Missinger's murderer, a charming socialite named Andrea Robinson.

Luckily, her blind spots hadn't burned her too much. She survived both those situations and even solved the cases. But she knew that much of that had been luck, which would eventually run out. Her gut could still play a role in investigations, but she was determined not to let it cloud her judgment or supersede the evidence.

And the evidence in front of her now was pretty clear: whoever had killed Penelope Wooten had a serious grudge. As they'd been informed, there were eight stab wounds, most quite deep. There were also defensive wounds on the palms that suggested Penelope had seen the attack coming.

Jessie pointed at them as she spoke.

"The person who did this could have stabbed her in the back but apparently wanted her to be frightened, to see what was about to happen. That suggests this was personal and not just some burglar panicking."

"Agreed," Ryan says. "This doesn't feel like a robbery gone wrong."

"No forced entry, right?" she double-checked with Brady.

"Correct."

"That's another sign that Penelope likely knew her assailant well enough to let him or her in," she mused, "assuming the culprit wasn't in the home already."

"The weapon appears to be the large butcher knife that's missing from the cutlery block on the kitchen counter," Ryan said, nodding in that direction. "That makes me suspicious that the murderer knew their DNA or fingerprints might be found on it."

"Another sign that this was a crime of passion," Jessie added. "If it had been preplanned, the perpetrator was more likely to have worn gloves."

"There's a Ring camera on the front door," Brady said. "We're trying to unlock her phone so we can access it. Those cameras are motion-activated so it won't show us everything. Still, maybe there's something there."

"Can't the husband show us the footage?" Ryan asked.

"He doesn't have it on his phone," Brady said. "She set the whole thing up."

"Can he at least give us the code to her phone?" Ryan wanted to know.

"He doesn't have that either. The passcode he had doesn't work. Apparently she changed it and never told him."

"That's not suspicious at all," Jessie said sarcastically.

"Don't jump to conclusions," Ryan warned, "especially with this case."

"Never," she assured him, smiling sweetly. "Bradenator, you said the kids are six and four. So they're likely in school or daycare right now. How did they get there?"

"Dad takes them in early on Tuesdays because of her yoga class. He said she wouldn't get back in time if she dropped them off."

"So she was here when they left for the morning?" she asked.

"He said she was asleep when he left with the children at six forty-five."

"He saw her sleeping?"

"I haven't talked to him yet," Brady said. "But he told the officer that when he rolled out of bed, she was lying next to him."

"So if he's telling the truth," Ryan mused, "that means the time of death was somewhere between six forty-five and eight a.m."

"If he's telling the truth," Brady agreed. "Of course, he could have offed her and then used the kids for an alibi."

"That's true," Jessie agreed. "But he would have had to have kept them out of the kitchen all morning. Sounds tricky. Plus, would the guy kill his own wife with his kids in the house? Whether it was him or someone else, it seems that the killer did this at a time when they knew the children wouldn't be a factor."

"That flies in the face of the 'crime of passion' theory," Ryan pointed out.

"Not necessarily," Jessie countered. "It's possible the killer came over for some other reason and things escalated. If so, the key is finding out what that reason was."

"Diplomatically," Brady reminded her, "without turning this into a media circus."

"Diplomatic is my middle name," Jessie assured him.

"It's a good thing you're not under oath," Ryan muttered under his breath, before adding out loud, "Let's interview some witnesses!"

CHAPTER ELEVEN

Jessie tried to hide her frustration.

Beth Copeland, the yoga teacher, wasn't much help. She was understandably rattled but even considering that, she just didn't seem to know much. She had arrived at exactly 8 a.m. as usual. She saw Eliza Longworth walk into the house as she pulled up.

"Are you sure she wasn't coming out of the house?" Jessie had asked.

"I thought she was going in. But now I'm not so sure."

She had discovered the body and started screaming. Eliza, who was looking for Penny upstairs, came running in and slipped on the blood. She tried to give her CPR even though Penny was obviously dead.

"Did she seem upset or could she have been faking it?" Brady had asked, more clunkily than Jessie would have liked.

"She seemed totally freaked out," Beth had answered. "I know they've been best friends since elementary school. Eliza lives on the next hill. She was devastated. I mean, she kept trying to resuscitate her, bawling the whole time, long after most people would have given up."

When they were satisfied they'd gotten everything they could, Brady authorized her to be taken to the hospital to get checked out. As they walked to the dining room where Colton Wooten was waiting, Jessie threw out a theory.

"Awful convenient that Eliza Longworth slipped in all that blood. Now she has a perfect excuse for having the victim's DNA all over her."

"Wow, you really have a dark view of humanity," Brady said.

"You're a detective with the Los Angeles Police Department," Jessie retorted with surprise. "Are you telling me you think most people are suffused with sweetness and light?"

"Of course not," he replied defensively. "But maybe we talk to her before drawing a conclusion like that."

"I'm not drawing any conclusions," Jessie said. "I'm just brainstorming. It's all a process, boys."

"Well, maybe we keep our ideas to ourselves when we interview the potential future district attorney," Brady suggested as they stepped into the living room.

"I think the FBI warped your soul," Ryan muttered to her quietly under his breath.

She was about to come back at him when she saw a crooked grin on his face and realized he was teasing her. There was no time anyway, as Colton Wooten was standing up to meet them.

The man was exactly what one would expect of a white-shoe lawyer with obvious political ambitions. Immaculately dressed in a three-piece navy suit, Wooten was at least two inches taller than Ryan and almost as chiseled. His thick, wavy black hair was parted down the side and his square jaw was set. He looked like a brunette Ken doll.

But there were a few cracks in the visage. His face was too perfectly tanned, as if it had been meticulously curated in a salon. There were blemishes on his cheeks, hidden by makeup, which Jessie recognized as mild Rosacea, often a sign of heavy drinking. And his eyes were extremely red. That could have been from crying, lack of sleep, or perhaps even stress after killing a loved one. He looked agitated, which wasn't unreasonable under the circumstances.

"I'm Detective Brady Bowen," Brady said, extending his hand as they approached. "We're terribly sorry for your loss, Mr. Wooten."

"It took you long enough to get to me," Wooten said, pointedly not shaking hands. "I've been sitting here forever. No one will tell me anything."

"We apologize for that, sir," Brady said, ignoring Wooten's tone. "As I'm sure you know better than most, it's important to get a sense of the crime scene early on, before anything might be disturbed. Unfortunately, that meant you had to wait longer than we would have liked. But we're here now. Do you mind if we ask you a few questions?"

"Only if I can ask you one first," he countered sharply.

"Of course," Brady said, though he was obviously taken aback.

Jessie was surprised at how confrontational Wooten was being. He didn't strike her as particularly grief-stricken. But, she reminded herself, people grieve in different ways. She was determined not to make snap judgments or let her gut alone guide her conclusions. Otherwise those ten weeks of FBI training would be for nothing.

Let the evidence guide you more than the husband's jerky demeanor.

"Why the hell has my wife's murder been assigned to a junior grade detective?" Wooten demanded. "I looked you up, Bowen. Your record isn't exactly overflowing with meritorious service commendations. And I don't even recognize these other two."

Jessie felt the urge to blurt something out but managed to force it down with a large gulp.

"Sir," Brady replied, doing his best to keep his voice level, "I was assigned to this case because I was available and, to be honest, because I have a reputation for discretion. The department knows that this is, in addition to being a tragedy, a delicate situation involving a high-profile public figure. My job is to keep it from becoming a circus."

Wooten looked at him for a long second and then, apparently satisfied with the answer, turned to Ryan and Jessie.

"What about these two?"

"This is Detective Ryan Hernandez. He actually works out of downtown but we've brought him in because of his experience in dealing with high-profile murder cases. He was instrumental in the capture of the serial killer Bolton Crutchfield, among others. We also used to be partners. I have great confidence in him."

"And the girl?" Wooten demanded dismissively.

Jessie's spine stiffened involuntarily and only an almost imperceptible head shake from Ryan kept her from kneeing the guy in the groin.

"This is Jessie Hunt, sir," Brady began. "She is among our most skilled forensic profilers. She has trained with the behavioral science team at the FBI and her track record is impeccable. She specializes in these kinds of cases and was specifically requested to assist on this one. She's an invaluable resource and we're lucky to have her."

Jessie stood there silently, shocked at what she'd heard. Not only did she barely recognize the description of herself, but nothing about Brady Bowen had led her to believe he was capable of coming up with it. Wooten sniffed in reluctant acceptance before saying.

"You had questions."

"Yes, sir," Brady said, diving in. "We've gone over your statement to the initial officer and just wanted to make sure you stand by all of it. Your wife was in bed sleeping when you got up at five thirty this morning and you believe she remained so when you left to take your children to school at six forty-five, is that correct?"

"It is."

Ryan piped up.

"No chance that, in your sleepy state as you got up, you mistook a rolled up comforter or pillows for your wife?"

"Not unless the pillows were snoring," Wooten answered. "She took a sleeping pill last night and she always sleeps heavily after that. I let her be."

"Did your wife take sleeping pills often?" Jessie asked.

"Sometimes," he replied, clearly irked by the question, "if she's stressed. Our son is autistic and occasionally the challenges of the day catch up with her. We all have our coping mechanisms."

His voice caught slightly at that last line but Jessie couldn't decide if it was a genuine moment of emotion or for show.

"Did your wife ever mention feeling threatened by anyone?" Brady asked.

"No."

"Had she recently had a falling out with anyone?"

"Not that I'm aware of."

"Mr. Wooten," Ryan said, "it's an open secret that you're seriously considering running for district attorney. How did your wife feel about that?"

"To be perfectly honest, she wasn't ecstatic about the idea. Things were stressful back when I worked in the prosecutor's office several years ago. They've settled down since I entered private practice. She was worried the strain of such a public job would be tough on the family, especially with Colt's challenges. He's doing really well since Eliza, her best friend, found his new school. But any dramatic change is hard for him. She had started to warm to the idea a bit. But that's the reason I hadn't announced anything yet. I wanted to make sure she was genuinely on board."

"Did you argue about it?" Jessie asked, looking at him closely.

"Sometimes," Wooten answered, meeting her stare with a glare of his own. "It wasn't an easy decision. Nothing in a marriage is easy. Are you married, Ms. Hunt?"

"Not anymore. It was too hard," she said, and then added without missing a beat, "Why didn't you know the password to her phone?"

"What?"

"When the officer asked for the phone code so he could access the Ring footage from your front door, you gave him an old one. Why didn't you have the current one?"

"She must have changed it and forgotten to tell me," he answered warily.

"Forgot or intentionally kept it from you?"

"What are you suggesting, Ms. Hunt?"

"I'm just asking a question, Mr. Wooten. Do you think her not telling you was an oversight or intentional? Did your wife keep many secrets from you?"

"Yeah," he snapped belligerently. "She was a swinger who loved key parties but didn't invite me because I'm too square. Is that what you want to hear?"

"Is that your answer, sir?" she demanded, not backing down an inch despite sensing the discomfort in the detectives near her.

"No," he said, relenting slightly. "Look, I don't know why she changed it without telling me. Maybe one of the kids saw her punch it in and was accessing the phone. That's happened before. Cole makes a habit of it. Frankly, I can't remember half the codes we have in this house. Maybe she figured it was just one more I'd forget. She probably would have been right. We had a good marriage. Not perfect, but good. I don't think she was keeping anything from me."

They asked a few more questions but all Wooten's answers were ones they had heard before or already knew the answers to. As Brady concluded the discussion with the standard promises to keep him in the loop, Ryan and Jessie walked back outside.

"What do you think?" he asked her.

"I think he's an asshole," Jessie replied.

"Thanks for the keen insight. What do you think of his story?"

"I don't know. I'm trying not to let his bad attitude color my opinion of the facts. I've been known to get rolled by charming personalities. I don't want to go too hard in the other direction with this guy. What do you think?"

"I want to see that Ring camera footage. I think it will really help us nail down the timeline more. And we should get the GPS data from his phone. Maybe that will offer a clue. As to his credibility, I just don't know. Hard to believe his wife just neglected to give him her phone code. If I did that, before the separation I mean, Shelly would have given me holy hell."

"Yeah," Jessie said, not wanting to probe that subject too deeply. "You know who almost certainly would know if Penelope Wooten was keeping secrets from her husband?"

"Who's that?"

"Her best friend since elementary school—
I say we pay her a visit at the hospital."

CHAPTER TWELVE

Eliza Longworth looked wiped out.

By the time Jessie, Ryan, and Brady got to her room at UCLA Medical Center in Santa Monica, she had showered and was resting in a bed with a tube in her arm. Her light brown hair, loose and straggly, blocked part of her face.

"I thought you requested she not be cleaned up," Jessie said to Brady more accusatorily than she intended.

"I did," he replied, looking at the doctor.

"I got your request but I made a command decision," the doctor told them as they peeked through the small rectangular window in the door to her room. "She was really hysterical for a while there—covered in her friend's blood, going on about how she could have saved her if she did CPR a little longer. We had to sedate her."

"Are we able to talk to her?" Ryan asked.

"Yes. She's only napping. But to the extent you can, please go easy on her. It was really taxing getting her to settle down. It would be great if you didn't rile her up again too much."

"We'll do our best," Brady assured him as they opened the door and stepped inside. The noise made Eliza stir slightly, though she didn't wake up.

"I'll do the honors," Ryan said, walking over to the bedside and speaking quietly. "Mrs. Longworth, can you please wake up? We need to speak with you."

Eliza repositioned herself slightly but her eyes remained closed. Ryan looked over at Jessie with an expression that suggested he was hesitant to push too hard. Jessie walked over and gave it a try.

"Mrs. Longworth," she said in a slightly louder voice than Ryan had used as she gently touched the woman's shoulder. "Please wake up. We need to talk to you."

The physical touch seemed to do the trick. The woman started slightly and her eyes snapped open.

"What?" she muttered, slightly disoriented.

"Mrs. Longworth," Jessie said, "we're with the Los Angeles Police Department. We need to ask you some questions about what happened this morning."

At those words, recognition seemed to fill Eliza's eyes. She settled back into the bed, her head collapsing on the pillow.

"Oh god, it was real," she moaned, clenching her eyes shut as if to push the memory away.

"I'm sorry to have to revisit what happened with you," Jessie said delicately. "But we need to get your statement while it's still fresh in your mind. Do you think you're up for that?"

Eliza Longworth squeezed her eyes even tighter than before, then suddenly opened them and nodded.

"Whatever it takes," she said, her voice now stronger than before.

"Okay," Jessie began. "I'm Jessie Hunt, a profiler with the LAPD. And these are Detectives Brady Bowen and Ryan Hernandez. We're investigating the case. Can you tell us what happened in your own words?"

Eliza forced herself to sit up slightly and took a moment to compose herself. Then she walked them through the particulars of what happened when she arrived at Penelope's house, from the moment she got there until the paramedics arrived. She had to stop a few times when describing the scene in the kitchen but eventually got through it.

"When was the last time you saw her before the kitchen?" Ryan asked.

"The previous day," Eliza said. "She was at my place for coffee around mid-morning."

"Did you notice anything unusual at that time?" Brady asked.

Eliza was silent for several seconds, as if weighing a big decision. Then she let out a huge sigh and nodded.

"I did," she said quietly.

"Please tell us," Brady said.

Eliza waited a moment, as if screwing up her courage. Then she dove in.

"We were on my balcony. When she went to get more coffee, she got a text on her phone. I glanced at it. It was from my husband, Gray. It revealed that … that, well, it showed that they'd been having an affair."

The three law enforcement officials stared at her open-mouthed, stunned at the revelation. Jessie realized that either Eliza was stunningly honest or the sedative she'd been given must be acting as some kind of inadvertent truth serum.

"For how long?" Ryan, the first to recover, asked.

"She said it was about a month."

"What happened after that?" he asked carefully.

"I freaked out. She said that she was ending it. But I told her she had betrayed my trust and that our friendship was over. I kicked her out. And then, when my husband got home that night, I kicked him out too."

"But you went over to her house the next morning," Jessie pointed out.

"Yes. You have to understand. We've been friends since third grade. We went to the same college. Our families go on vacations together. Our daughters are best friends. So, after a long night in which I didn't sleep, I made a decision. I couldn't just throw all of that away without trying to find a way to forgive her. She had told me she hadn't seen him in three days and that she was planning to break it off. I texted but she didn't reply. So I decided to go over there and face things head on. We had a yoga class scheduled for later that morning. I hoped to talk to her before Beth arrived, to say we could discuss things after the lesson. But I couldn't find her and … you know the rest."

"So you were just going to give her a pass for sleeping with your husband for the last month?" Jessie asked incredulously.

Eliza looked at her indignantly.

"No way," she insisted. "I felt like, well, if you want to know the truth, I felt like killing her. I know I shouldn't say that, but it's true. And yet, she's like a sister to me. I'm an only child but it never felt that way because of Penny. What was I supposed to do—just pretend like the last twenty-five years of our lives together were meaningless? I had to try to find a way past it."

"Let me get clarification on something," Jessie said, refusing to allow herself to be swayed by the emotion of the moment. "When Beth arrived, were you going into the house for the first time or coming out?"

"I was going in. I saw Beth pull up and I wanted to get in to talk to Penny, even if only for a few seconds. Otherwise it would have just been too awkward, going through an hour-long yoga session with this unspoken thing between us."

"But you couldn't find her?"

"No, I only got to the living room before Beth walked in. We were calling out for Penny. I thought maybe she was upstairs and started to go look when Beth started screaming from the kitchen. That's...that's when..."

She trailed off, unable to continue. Ryan switched topics quickly in the hopes of keeping her from losing it completely.

"Did her husband know about the affair?" he asked.

Eliza managed to pull herself together. Sitting fully upright now, she pushed the bed sheet off her body to reveal she was wearing only a hospital gown. There was an ugly bruise on Eliza's right knee where she must have hit the kitchen tile after slipping on the blood.

Jessie couldn't help but notice that the woman's body had a toned wiriness to it that suggested yoga wasn't the only part of her regular workout routine. Penelope Wooten was much taller, but model thin. Eliza was clearly an athlete. It wasn't hard to picture this smaller but more muscular woman physically overwhelming her.

"I genuinely don't know," Eliza said, sliding her legs over the side of the bed. "A day ago, I would have said she'd tell me everything. But now I don't know what she kept from whom. Colton is a pretty well-known lawyer. I don't know if I'm speaking out of school but he was thinking of running for office. I'm sure this would have complicated things. She might have wanted to keep it from him for that reason alone."

"But she never hinted at problems in their marriage?" Brady asked.

"She said they went to counseling and that it helped. But she told me it was for the usual stuff—lack of communication, that kind of thing. She even suggested that Gray and I go because I was complaining that he'd become distant. Of course, now I see that in a different light."

"You said Penelope was going to break it off with your husband, that she hadn't been in contact with him for three days?" Jessie said.

"That's what she told me."

"Do you know if she actually did that? Broke it off?"

"Yes. When I confronted Gray that night, he said that she told him it was over and that he'd agreed."

"Did he seem angry about that?" Brady asked.

"Angry that it was over or angry that he'd been found out?"

"Whichever?" Brady said.

"He was angry, to the extent that he shows that sort of thing. Gray's not exactly the 'scream and shout' type. He's very ... retiring. But in his own way, he was definitely upset. I don't know if it was because he was busted, because he didn't get to nail her anymore, or because I was kicking him out. My guess is that it was a combination of all of it."

"Do you know where he went after he left your house?" Jessie asked.

"To a hotel, I assume. I haven't talked to him since last night."

"Not even to tell him about Penelope's passing?" Jessie pressed.

Eliza looked at her in amazement.

"I've been a little busy," she said.

Just then the door opened and a nurse walked in.

"Mrs. Longworth," she said, clearly perturbed, "please don't try to get out of bed. You're medicated and have an IV. We don't want you falling."

"Sorry," Eliza said absently. She tried to lift her feet back into the bed but struggled so Brady gave her a hand.

"I know you're doing an investigation," the nurse said to the three of them, "but Mrs. Longworth really needs to get as much rest as possible. Do you think you could resume your questioning later?"

"That's okay," Brady said. "I think we're good for now. However, we may want to speak to speak to you a bit later, Mrs. Longworth. Here's my card if you think of anything else in the interim."

He placed the card on the small table beside the bed and they all shuffled out as the nurse pulled the sheet back over Eliza.

"Initial thoughts?" Brady asked as they walked down the hall to the elevator.

"She's got motive," Jessie said. "Her best friend betrayed their lifelong friendship by screwing her husband. It doesn't get much more clear-cut than that."

"I don't know," Ryan countered. "There's also a wronged husband, especially one who might be worried that his run for office was about to get derailed by a personal scandal. That strikes me as a fairly compelling motive as well."

Brady shook his head.

"I see you that and raise you the cheating husband who just had his life explode and can't be enthused with the woman who admitted their fling to his wife."

"Yeah, we should maybe talk to that guy," Ryan agreed. "It sounds like we have a potpourri of credible suspects."

"We also need to go back and talk to Wooten," Brady said. "Either he's lying or he's pretty clueless for a guy who used to be a prosecutor. Are we really supposed to believe he had no idea this was going on right under his nose?"

"You might be surprised," Jessie cautioned. "Sometimes people can be shockingly blind to the secrets of the people closest to them, the people they love."

Neither Brady nor Ryan responded, though both knew what relationship she was referencing. Jessie was grateful for their tact.

As they rode down in the elevator, an image flashed through her mind of obliviously lying in bed next to her then-husband, Kyle. It was quickly replaced by one of him in a gray jumpsuit, taunting her from behind a glass partition in the prison where he was incarcerated.

Everybody has secrets. Some of us are just better at hiding them.

CHAPTER THIRTEEN

Jessie had been outvoted.

She wanted to interview Gray Longworth first, before he had too much time to formulate answers to questions about Penny's death. Assuming they were breaking the news to him, she wanted to study his reaction to it. The longer they waited, the more likely he'd be able to prepare for their arrival.

But Brady was adamant that they needed to go back to Colton Wooten and let him clarify his statement. If he spoke to the press before they had time to confront him about his wife's affair, the very media circus they were trying to avoid might be inevitable.

Ryan saw the merits of both arguments but ultimately deferred to Brady, who was the lead detective on the case. He was the one who would face the heat from his superiors if things went sideways so it seemed only fair that he should make the final call.

Since they all agreed that they shouldn't split up, that meant their next stop was to the offices of Wooten & Camby, LLC, where Colton was apparently hunkered down. They parked in the garage below the gleaming Santa Monica tower where his practice was headquartered. As they rode up to the twenty-second-floor office in a glass elevator, Brady got a call.

"It's the station," he said as he answered. "I'll put it on speaker."

"Detective Bowen?" asked the young-sounding female voice on the phone.

"Yes," he answered with a smile as he mouthed the word "rookie" to them. "Is this Officer Mueller?"

"Yes sir. I have a few updates in regard to the issues you wanted pursued."

"Go ahead, Mueller."

"We have the GPS data for Colton Wooten's phone as well as the Ring footage from this morning."

"What about the location data on Eliza and Gray Longworth?" he asked.

"We're still waiting for that," she said. "It should be available within the hour. Would you like me to send you the camera footage now?"

"That would be great, Mueller," he said as the elevator door opened and the three of them stepped out into the hallway of the twenty-second floor. "In the meantime, what did the GPS show?"

"According to the location data, Mr. Wooten left his home at six forty-three a.m. He stopped at the Palisades Friends Preschool at six fifty-two and left again at seven oh-one. His next stop was Mendocino School for Strivers at seven thirteen. And that's it."

"What do you mean, 'that's it'?" Brady demanded.

"After that, the signal disappears. There's no way to know if the phone died or was turned off intentionally. It was activated again at eight twenty-two a.m."

"Where was he then?"

"At his Santa Monica office," Mueller said.

"So his whereabouts are unknown for over an hour?"

"It would seem so."

"What about the GPS in his car?" Jessie asked.

"We're working on that. But that requires jumping through a few hoops and the chief wants us to be ... delicate in how we handle the requests."

"Understood," Bowen said. "I see the Ring footage just came in. Thanks, Mueller. We have to go but keep me apprised of any updates."

"Yes, sir," Mueller said, sounding relieved that she wasn't being personally blamed for the car location data delay.

After hanging up, Brady was just about to play the doorbell video footage when a young man in a fancy suit walked past them.

"You know," he said after the man had passed them, "maybe we go somewhere a little more private to look at this."

They all went to the opposite end of the hall from Wooten's office, and around the corner near the emergency exit. Jessie and Ryan crowded around him as he hit play.

The motion-activated footage showed Eliza Longworth at the front door of the house.

"Penny!" they heard her yell. "Beth's here. Are we still on for yoga?"

She rang the doorbell and tried again. The footage wasn't the best quality but to Jessie at least, she didn't seem to be acting suspiciously. Maybe a little nervous, but that could be easily explained by the nature of the situation. She was there, after all, to discuss moving on after her best friend slept with her husband.

"Penny, can I come in? We should talk for a sec before Beth arrives."

After waiting a few more seconds, Eliza tried the front door, which was unlocked.

"Penny," they heard her shout from somewhere inside, her voice getting more distant with each second. "You left the door unlocked. Beth's pulling up. Did you get my text? Can we talk privately for a minute before we start?"

A few seconds later Beth walked through the open door, calling out, "Ladies, I'm here!"

The two women spoke briefly and, though it was hard to catch the actual content of their conversation, neither sounded especially distressed.

About thirty seconds later the screaming began.

"Well," Brady said when it ended, "I don't know how helpful that was other than to confirm everything we already suspected."

"We did get clarity on one thing," Ryan noted. "This shows that Eliza was going into the house, not coming out, when Beth arrived.

It doesn't completely absolve her but at least her story is holding up so far."

"Yeah, but she knew that camera was on the doorbell. That whole thing could have been for show," Jessie countered, though it was becoming increasingly hard to make the case.

"You really have it in for this woman," Brady said. "Why?"

"I'm just covering all the bases," Jessie replied, ignoring the skeptical look she saw Ryan give her out of the corner of his eye.

"Let's set that aside for the time being," Ryan said, not commenting on the veracity of her assertion. "For now, let's focus on the man we came here to see. He's got some explaining to do himself."

Brady seemed satisfied with that plan and headed down the hall toward Wooten & Camby. As Jessie started to follow, Ryan put his hand on her shoulder and gently pulled her aside.

"When we get some private time, you are going to tell me what the hell is going on with you."

And before she could reply, he was halfway down the hall.

CHAPTER FOURTEEN

Wooten made them wait twenty minutes.

Jessie thought it was odd that he would keep the people investigating his wife's murder cooling their heels. But she kept that to herself when they were finally ushered into his office. Along the way down the hall, she noticed several very familiar-looking pieces of artwork behind heavy glass. She wondered if they were the originals and briefly regretted not paying closer attention in her art history class.

When they were led into Wooten's corner all-glass office, he was on a call, standing jacket-less with his back to them. His assistant got his attention, pointed out the three law enforcement officials in the room, and left. Wooten spoke for another thirty seconds before hanging up.

"Any updates?" he asked them without preamble.

"Some actually," Brady said. "Care to take a seat?"

"I prefer to stand."

Jessie, vaguely irked by his attitude, decided to take the initiative and sat down in one of the chairs across the desk from him.

"I was surprised to hear you'd be in the office, Mr. Wooten," she said. "I'd have thought you would want to take a personal day."

"Unfortunately, it's not as simple as that. I have a number of clients in court proceedings today and the justice system doesn't grind to a halt just because my world is falling apart."

"You couldn't get continuances?"

"In most cases, yes," he said. "But one criminal trial is currently with the jury and we had a deposition in a high-profile civil case.

Those had to be farmed out to the right people. I don't know how long I will be gone from work and I want to make sure each client is placed with the appropriate replacement."

"Your professional dedication is admirable," she said with just the tiniest hint of skepticism.

He either didn't notice or pretended not to.

"The truth is," he said, "there's not much else I can do right now. And in a weird way, it's keeping me sane. Focusing on the legal minutiae keeps my mind from going to darker places. Plus, this is my only window to get stuff done. Once I pick up the kids later, everything else will take a back seat. I'm not sure how I'm going to break it to them. Ana will be hard enough. She's only four. But Colt—I don't know how that will work. Forget the emotional fallout for a second. His mother is central to his routine. And without that routine, he tends to ... struggle."

"I'm terribly sorry, Mr. Wooten," Brady said, sounding genuinely sympathetic. "We'll do our best to be quick here so you can get back to resolving those matters. We have just a few additional questions for you."

"I thought you said you had updates," Wooten reminded him.

"Updates *and* questions," Brady replied innocuously. "The first thing is, we were a little confused about where you went after you dropped off your children this morning."

"I came straight here. Why?"

"Did you turn off your phone, sir?" Ryan asked, not answering Wooten's question.

"No. It died. I didn't have my charger with me so I couldn't plug it in until I got here."

"But your last stop, your son's school, is less than twenty minutes from here," Ryan noted. "And yet your phone was off for over an hour."

Wooten looked at him with an air of impatience but forced himself to answer the question.

"I got pulled into an early meeting and forgot about the phone until I got out. What is this all about?"

"We're just trying to establish a timeline for everyone," Brady said, jumping in.

"Who else's timeline are you looking at?" Wooten asked.

"Well, we just spoke to Eliza Longworth at the hospital and got hers," Jessie volunteered, knowing what she was about to say could have serious consequences. "While we were there, she also told us your wife was having an affair with her husband. Is there any reason *you* didn't volunteer that information to us?"

Jessie watched him closely, looking for any reaction that might reveal something unintended. Wooten looked back at her with squinty, penetrating eyes. He did not seem shocked by her question.

"Yes, there is, Ms. Hunt. In addition to being shell-shocked over her death, I was embarrassed. I know that shouldn't have been my priority this morning. But it played a role. I just found out that my wife had been carrying on an affair with not just someone I knew, not just our neighbor, but her best friend's husband. It was a lot to process. And I guess I didn't handle it as well as I could have."

"You lied to us, Mr. Wooten," Jessie persisted.

"No, I said we had a good marriage. I said she wasn't keeping anything from me, which is true. She had already told me about the affair before this happened—yesterday actually. I didn't spill my guts to you but I didn't lie either."

"How did you feel when she told you?" Ryan asked.

"How do you think I felt, Detective? I was devastated. I was pissed off. I felt betrayed. In general, I felt like my whole world was collapsing."

"Because this would hurt your attempt to run for district attorney?" Jessie pressed.

Wooten again glared at her and again remained composed as he answered.

"I'm not going to deny that was a factor," he admitted. "But that wasn't the main thing. Even the cheating itself wasn't the main thing."

"What was?" Ryan asked.

"It was so ... unsettling. Penny is the rock in our family. She pays the bills. She volunteers at both kids' schools. Hell, as you saw, she even handled the codes for the security cameras. The idea that she would do something so reckless, that she was so unmoored—it really messed with my whole conception of who she is."

"But she told you she was ending it?" Brady prompted, apparently trying to get away from feelings and back to hard facts.

"She didn't just tell me, she showed me."

"What do you mean?"

"She texted him while I was with her," he replied. "I watched her type out the message."

"What did it say?" Brady asked.

"I don't remember the exact words. You can check her phone for that. But the gist of it was, 'This is over. I told Colton. I told Eliza. We have to face the consequences of what we've done.'"

"Did he respond?" Jessie asked.

"Yeah," Wooten said, shaking his head at the memory of it. "I thought he'd give some milquetoast reply, whether he accepted what she said or tried to change her mind. Gray's kind of a milquetoast guy."

"But he didn't?" Ryan said.

"No. He came back hard. He demanded to know how she could do that without talking to him first. He called her a bitch. He said she had ruined his life. I was surprised. He's usually such a timid guy. Even under the circumstances, it seemed out of character for him."

"Did you reach out to him after that?" Jessie asked.

"What? To defend my wife's honor? Nothing he said was wrong, if you ask me. Besides, it's not like I was going to go there and fight the guy. I knew that he'd get what he deserved from Eliza. She would crush him."

"Is Eliza the 'crushing' type?' Ryan asked.

"All I know is, as pissed as I was, you can probably double it for her. She and Penny have known each other forever. They swapped juice boxes in grade school. And then her own husband made a move on Penny. It can't have been pretty."

"Was it pretty in your house?" Jessie wondered.

"It wasn't as ugly as you might think. Because of Colt, screaming matches aren't really an option in our home. If we start yelling at each other, he melts down. Escalating any situation only makes it worse. And by the time he and Ana went to bed, Penny had taken her sleeping pill. She wasn't in a place to hash things out. So I decided to let it lie for a day. I figured things would be clearer today. That worked out great."

The detectives were all silent for several seconds, not sure how to respond to Colton Wooten's reaction to his wife's death.

"I assume you won't mind us checking your car's GPS data," Brady finally said, "to confirm your whereabouts this morning."

"My alibi, you mean?" he replied caustically. "I assumed you already had."

Ten minutes later, they stepped out of the glass elevator and walked through the building's lobby to the parking structure across the street.

"Did you even *consider* arresting him?" Jessie asked Brady, unable to contain the frustration that had been building up since they left Wooten's office.

"On what grounds?" he asked indignantly.

"His alibi is questionable at best. He wasn't honest about his wife's affair and he's got a perfect motive."

Brady looked at her with self-righteous exasperation.

"His alibi will either be proved or disproved within the hour. Not mentioning the affair in an initial interview, while suspicious, isn't a crime. He wasn't under oath. And he's one of at least three people with a solid motive. We need something more definitive than that to take him into custody."

"Are you sure those are the reasons?" she needled.

"Just to be clear, you seem to be suggesting that I didn't cuff him back there because he's running for DA, right? Do you really think, after what I just laid out, that doing so would have been the wisest course of action?"

"I'm just trying to make sure your top priority is solving this case and not avoiding a scandal."

"With all due respect, Jessie, I think I can do both," he said, stopping. "I'm going to check in with the station. You two go ahead. I'll meet you at the car."

He pulled out his phone as Jessie and Ryan continued walking to the parking structure.

"Something on your mind?" Ryan asked when they were out of earshot.

"What do you mean?" Jessie asked.

"First you treated Eliza Longworth like she was an ex-con out on parole. Then you pushed for a former prosecutor to be arrested in his office. And now you go after Brady. It seems like you're ready to throw everyone behind bars today."

Jessie stopped at and stared at him, frustrated by his comments.

"You don't think I'm just employing some professional skepticism?"

"I think it goes a little beyond that," Ryan said. "Skepticism is good. In fact, it's essential in our line of work. But you still have to be open to the possibility that people are occasionally telling you the truth."

Jessie resumed walking, trying to take in his words without absorbing any judgment.

"I guess I've just been burned a lot by assuming the best in people," she said slowly. "It happened with Kyle and again with the Andrea Robinson case, so I'm just trying to stay objective. With Eliza Longworth, I recognize her situation. Hell, I was *in* her situation. So I feel a connection to her. I don't want that to cloud my judgment so I have to be hard on her. Maybe I was too hard. And then, to be fair to her, I had to be equally harsh on Wooten. And since he was such a jerk, that came easily, maybe too easy. I don't know. Maybe all that FBI training messed me up."

"Or," Ryan countered, "maybe you're just a little nervous and rusty because you haven't done this in a live situation in a few months."

"Maybe," Jessie admitted.

"So cut yourself a little slack. Just don't cut up every person we interview in the process. Sound good?"

"Sounds goo—" Jessie started to say, before being cut off by a loud popping sound less than a hundred feet away.

She reached for her sidearm, then remembering she didn't have one yet, dropped to the ground, lying prone on the parking garage cement. After about five seconds of silence, she looked up at Ryan. He was staring down at her with a stunned look on his face.

"I'm pretty sure it was just a backfire," he said.

"You're probably right," she said, sheepishly getting back to her feet. "Still, better safe than sorry."

"Really?" he said, dubious. "That struck me as more than just caution. You've been skittish all day. You want to tell me what has you so sketched out?"

"Just 'first day back' jitters, I guess."

"I don't believe that for one second," he said.

In the distance, Jessie saw Brady walking toward them.

"Let it lie for now," she said quietly. "I'll fill you in later."

"Please," Ryan insisted, "because this can't continue."

Jessie nodded even as she wondered how she would broach the subject.

Yeah, maybe at lunch over a ham and cheese sandwich I'll tell you how my serial killer dad is currently hunting down my address.

CHAPTER FIFTEEN

Jessie's suspect list seemed to be in constant flux.

They were just arriving at Gray Longworth's commercial real estate brokerage firm in Venice when Brady got a call from Officer Mueller. This time, he didn't put it on speaker. After about thirty seconds, he hung up.

"Got some news," he said.

"We kind of figured, Brady," Ryan replied. "Good or bad?"

"Depends on who you are. I'm guessing Colt Jr. and Anastasia will be happy about it. We got the details of Wooten's vehicle GPS data. It shows that he arrived at work when he said he did. We also checked the security footage from his building. It shows him entering but not leaving."

"Couldn't he have snuck out some alternate exit and taken a rideshare back to the house?" Jessie asked.

"I suppose it's technically possible," Brady answered. "But that gives him a really small window to get there, kill his wife, and return to work in time for his meeting."

"Fair point," Jessie acknowledged, noting Brady's surprise at her willingness to concede the argument. "So maybe we put him in the 'unlikely' bucket of suspects."

"Yeah," Ryan agreed as he pulled into a street parking spot. "But let's not eliminate him completely. He could have hired someone. A former prosecutor would know people willing to do that kind of work. I'm not ready to cross him off just yet."

They got out and walked the half block to Longworth's office. Considering he was in commercial real estate, the building was surprisingly uninspiring. Composed mostly of dull, eggshell-colored concrete, it looked particularly out of place situated in the middle of this funky section of Venice. Along the short walk from the car to his office, they passed a vegan restaurant, an organic clothing store, and a marijuana dispensary. His building stood out by not standing out.

They entered the lobby, where Ryan flashed his badge at the receptionist.

"We need to speak to Gray Longworth," he said tersely.

The woman looked taken aback and glanced at a spiral notebook on the desk in front of her.

"It appears he's in a meeting right now. I'll let him know when it's over. Please have a seat."

"His meeting's over," Ryan said firmly. "Please show us to his office now."

Despite clearly being flustered, the receptionist did as she was asked. Ryan took the lead. As Jessie and Brady trailed behind, she leaned over and muttered to him.

"I think I can guess who played good cop and who played bad cop when you interrogated suspects."

"We had our roles," Brady conceded. "But in this case I think Ryan just wants to get in there and question Longworth before the guy has a chance to prepare himself."

"Prepare himself for what?"

"For learning of Penelope Wooten's death. Unlike you, I'm no profiler, so I need pretty overt visual cues to tell me if a suspect is genuinely surprised by news or is faking. This should help with that."

They reached Longworth's office, which was separated from the long hallway by a glass wall and door. He was on the phone and looked up when the receptionist opened the door.

"Mr. Longworth," she said, "these detectives are here to speak with you."

He stared as the three of them filed into the room one after the other. After a moment of mutual silence, he spoke into the phone.

"I'll have to call you back," he said. "Something … came up."

He hung up and continued staring at them, his expression a mix of confusion and apprehension.

Jessie gave him a once-over. Gray Longworth wasn't a large man, maybe no taller than his wife. His blond hair was wispy and his fair skin looked like it might not survive a half hour in the sun. And yet there was something about him that made Jessie get why Eliza might go for him.

Despite Colton Wooten's description of him as milquetoast, he carried himself with a hint of mischievousness that was intriguing. She imagined it was more pronounced when he wasn't facing three members of law enforcement.

"May we sit?" Ryan asked, though it didn't sound like he needed permission.

Longworth nodded and all three of them took seats opposite him.

"What can I do for you, officers?" he asked hesitantly.

"Detectives, actually," Ryan said. "We need to ask you a few questions about Penelope Wooten."

At the sound of her name Gray Longworth's eyes grew as large as saucers.

"What about her?' he asked, his voice quavering, all hint of roguishness disappearing.

"Before we begin our questions, is there anything you want to tell us?"

Jessie saw what Ryan was doing. Longworth seemed shaken. If he didn't know exactly what the police were aware of, maybe he'd inadvertently reveal something they didn't know yet. Longworth looked on the verge of panic, as if he were weighing some momentous decision. Finally, he spoke.

"I didn't mean to do it."

There was a moment of silence in which Jessie wondered if Ryan might give the man his Miranda rights. If he was about to confess, they'd want that out of the way.

"Didn't mean to do what?" Ryan asked slowly.

"To send that text," he answered. "The second I sent it, I wished I could retract it. You have to understand. I was upset. She'd just told me that she'd revealed everything to my wife. I could see my whole world collapsing around me. So I lashed out. It was wrong, I know. But is really it a crime?"

"Mr. Longworth," Brady said, speaking for the first time, "are you telling us that your only admission at this time is to sending a nasty text?"

"No," Longworth replied. "I mean, I'm also admitting to the affair. But I *know* that's not a crime. I didn't think the text was either. Did she file a restraining order or something? Because it's not necessary."

"Mr. Longworth," Ryan said, ignoring the question, "where were you this morning between the hours of six and eight a.m.?"

"What? I don't know. Why?" Longworth asked, flustered.

"Just answer the question, please."

"Don't you have to tell me what this is all about?" he demanded, standing up. The quaver had returned to his voice but now it was mixed with petulant indignation. "It sounds like you are asking me for an alibi. I feel like you aren't being straight with me."

"I'm just asking you a question, Mr. Longworth," Ryan said. "Are you refusing to answer me? Because a man who has nothing to hide probably wouldn't react to a simple question in this manner."

Gray Longworth stepped out from behind his desk and walked across the room to open the glass door.

"Please leave," he said, holding it open.

Jessie couldn't help but notice that he was not living up to his milquetoast reputation.

"It doesn't work like that, Mr. Longworth," Ryan said, not moving an inch. "Now if you are refusing to answer questions, that's your right. In fact, I'm about to list a whole series of rights to you, including your right to an attorney. But if I take that step, it means I'm about to take you into custody. Is that the step you want me to take?"

"Take me into custody for what?" Longworth said belligerently, getting dangerously close to Ryan. "For not wanting to chat about how my marriage might be over because I was screwing my wife's best friend?"

"No, Mr. Longworth. I'd take you into custody on suspicion of murdering your wife's best friend."

"Wait? What?"

This was the moment Jessie had been waiting for. Gray Longworth's face was the picture of shock. His hostile demeanor morphed into crestfallen dismay. The problem was, Jessie couldn't be sure if he was surprised that Penelope Wooten was dead, that he was potentially being arrested for it, or if he was faking the whole thing.

"Do I need to cuff you Mr. Longworth," Ryan persisted, "or are you willing to answer my questions?"

"Penny's dead?" he asked, sounding as if he hadn't completely understood.

"She is," Ryan assured him. "Does that come as a surprise to you?"

Longworth's expression changed suddenly from alarm to rage. His face turned red.

"How dare you ..." he started to shout as he shoved both hands into Ryan's chest.

It was a mistake. Ryan was half a head taller and forty pounds heavier than Longworth. He was also trained in close quarters combat. It took about four seconds for him to knock Longworth's arms away, knee him in the groin, shove him to the ground face first, put his knee in the small of the man's back, and slap handcuffs on him.

"Need a hand?" Brady asked, amused.

"I'm good," Ryan replied, before reading Longworth his rights. When he was done, he pulled the man to his feet and led him out of the office.

"You can't do this," Longworth protested. "I haven't done anything wrong."

"You assaulted a law enforcement officer," Brady noted as they walked down the hall. "If you don't think that's wrong, I'm worried about what else you consider within the bounds of appropriate behavior."

Jessie wondered the same thing.

CHAPTER SIXTEEN

Jessie didn't know what to make of Gray Longworth.

As she stared at him through the one-way mirror of an interrogation room at West L.A. Station, she couldn't tell if his nervous sweating was due to general anxiety at his situation or fear of getting busted for something far worse than shoving a cop.

"You ready?" Ryan asked, poking his head in. "I think we've let him stew long enough."

"What has it been, thirty minutes?" she asked. "And he still hasn't asked for a lawyer?"

"Nope. And he's offering to talk too. Brady thinks he's hoping he can get me to drop the assault charge if he charms me."

"Can he?" Jessie asked.

"I'm happy to let him think so if it turns him into a Chatty Cathy."

"So do we have a plan of action?"

"I say we let him vent a little. He'll probably want to justify himself. Brady will appear sympathetic to that so that he's more forthcoming."

"In that case," Jessie suggested, "maybe I should hang in here for a little bit. Having a woman in there about his wife's age might make him feel more judged than he would otherwise. Give me a signal when you're really ready to bear down on him and I'll join the party. Maybe seeing me walk in will get him sweating more than he already is."

"Sounds good," Ryan agreed and closed the door.

Jessie pulled out a chair and settled in as if she were preparing to watch a movie. Only for this screening she had a pen, a pad of paper, and the knowledge that she would soon be talking to the main character.

A few seconds later, Brady and Ryan walked in and sat across the table from Longworth. No one spoke for several seconds. Eventually, Ryan leaned forward and spoke in almost a whisper.

"You know, the way you came at me back at your office doesn't really jibe with the way Colton Wooten described you."

Longworth squirmed in his chair, as if struggling with whether or not to respond. Eventually it became clear that he wouldn't be able to stop himself.

"What did he say?" he finally asked.

"He said you were a milquetoast kind of guy."

"Yeah, well, Colt can shove it where the sun doesn't shine."

"Whoa," Ryan said, feigning surprise. "Sounds like there might be a little animosity there. That must have been fun on your dual family trips."

"I guess we won't be having any more of those," Longworth replied.

The comment sat there in all its ugliness for a good while before he tried to clean it up.

"I just mean ..." he started.

"I think we know what you mean, Gray," Ryan interrupted. "You don't mind if I call you Gray?"

"Actually, I prefer ..."

"So Gray," Ryan continued, blowing through Longworth's protestation, "we've established that you're not as bland as Wooten thinks, that you aren't super fond of him, that you were sleeping with his wife, and that you don't seem all that broken up over her death."

"That's not true," Longworth protested, trying to stand up but prevented by the cuffs attaching his hand to the table leg.

"You just made a crack about family vacations," Ryan noted. "That strikes me as pretty callous."

"I didn't mean it like that."

"But you have to admit," Brady chimed in, sounding sympathetic, "that sounded kind of cold. You don't seem very devastated about Penelope's death."

"I'm still in shock. A person I was involved with is dead and I'm sitting in a police station, handcuffed, being asked about it. I haven't had much time to process what happened to her, what with trying to prove that I wasn't involved in it."

"Fair enough," Brady said generously. "Then maybe you can answer the question we were trying to get resolved back at your office—where were you between the hours of six and eight a.m.?"

Longworth sat still for a moment, his face scrunched up as if he were trying to recall. Jessie found it unconvincing that he would be struggling to remember something that happened less than eight hours earlier.

"I spent the night in a hotel. This morning I came back to our neighborhood, parked on the street a block from our house, and went for a run on a nearby trail. After the run, when I knew Eliza had taken the kids to school, I went to the house to try to shower, change, and grab some fresh clothes. But she had changed the locks. So I went to my gym to clean up. Then I came into work."

"Did you take your phone with you on your run?" Brady asked.

"No, I didn't have the armband I use to hold it so I just left it in the car."

"How long was the run?"

"I don't know the exact mileage," Longworth said. "But I'd guess about five miles. I know it was less than an hour."

"Mr. Longworth," Brady asked, almost apologetically, "would you be willing to hand over your phone so we can confirm its location at that time using its GPS data?"

Jessie stood up. Ryan hadn't motioned for her but she saw an opportunity and wasn't going to wait for permission to take advantage of it. As she walked out, she heard Longworth answer.

"I don't have a problem with that," he said.

She stepped over to the interrogation room door, knocked, and poked her head in.

"Mind if I join you for a moment?" she asked.

"Be our guest," Brady said, as if inviting her to a dinner party.

"Thanks so much," Jessie said as she walked over. Ryan instinctively got up and she took his chair, moving it so that she was only two feet away from Longworth.

"Hi, Mr. Longworth," she said, her voice all sweetness and light. "We haven't actually spoken yet. But I have a question for you. Would that be all right?"

"Of course," he answered, though he looked uncomfortable with how close she was.

"Great. I was just wondering why, in your text message to Penny, you called her a bitch?"

"I didn't... did I...?" he said, then started over. "Listen, I was upset. I just found out that my whole life had been blown up. I lashed out. I said some stuff I regret now."

"You were pretty angry with her, huh? For blowing up your whole life?"

"In that moment, sure—I was upset. But it doesn't mean ..."

"You knew Eliza was going to be pissed, right?" she said, mowing over him and leaning in close so that their faces were only inches apart. "You knew that what you'd done was far worse than stepping out with some escort, didn't you? This was your wife's best friend since they played with dolls and had slumber parties. It was unforgivable. There was no way you could repair it. That must have been so frustrating, to watch your perfect life disintegrating right before your eyes. Isn't that right, Gray?"

Longworth took a deep breath, as if trying to suck in an extra reservoir of patience. It didn't seem to work.

"She could have just ended it," he blurted out. "She didn't have to tell everyone. Now two families' lives are ruined because of what she did."

"Because of what *she* did?" Jessie repeated. "Did she tie you down and force you to cheat on your wife? Were you a passive observer in this process? Were you the victim, Gray?"

Longworth shook his head in frustration, inadvertently bumping Jessie in the nose with the crown of his head. Going with it, she threw her weight backward and toppled off the chair, crumbling in a heap on the ground.

She looked up at him, feigning shock and a bit of fear. He looked completely discombobulated, as if he hadn't totally grasped what had happened.

"I didn't mean to …"

Ryan aggressively jumped between them.

"You just assaulted a law enforcement officer for the second time in less than two hours, Mr. Longworth," he said. "While Detective Bowen attends to her, I'm going to accompany you to one of our cells, where you are less likely to harm anyone else."

Within ten seconds, Longworth was uncuffed from the table and hurried out of the room. He was already halfway down the hall when Jessie heard him plaintively plead, "It was an accident."

"Swift thinking," Brady said. "I think we would have had to let him go soon if he hadn't 'assaulted' you like that."

"Thanks. But it will probably only buy us a day. He'll be out tomorrow for sure. We need to use that window to see if he's more than just an asshole."

"What do you think?" Brady asked her as he offered a hand.

"I think he's got a lot of pent up anger," Jessie said as pulled her up. "The question is, was he mad enough to kill?"

CHAPTER SEVENTEEN

"So, are you ready to tell me what's up with you now?"

Ryan asked her the question on their mid-afternoon drive back to Central Station. Both of them, having missed the seafood lunch he promised, were shoving gas station sandwiches into their mouths.

Longworth was in custody overnight. Officers tailing both Colton Wooten and Eliza Longworth reported that neither was acting unusually. Colton was still at work and Eliza, after being released from the hospital, had picked up her children and gone home. It wasn't clear that she even knew her husband was under arrest.

Gray Longworth's phone and car GPS data confirmed that both were in the same spot from 6:18 to 7:27 a.m. After that, they moved to his house briefly, and then his office. There was no official way to confirm where he was during that hour. But tomorrow morning officers planned to canvass the running trail to ask if other joggers had seen him. In the meantime, they could keep him locked up for at least twenty-four hours.

The preliminary coroner's report wouldn't be available until tomorrow either. So there was no reason to stay on the west side. After promising Brady they'd return in the morning, they headed back downtown, which was when Ryan began his own interrogation.

"What do you mean?" Jessie asked, playing for time.

"No games, please," he insisted. "You promised that you'd tell me why you've been so jumpy today. You almost leapt through the roof of the car when that vagrant tapped on your window this morning. And later on, you dropped to the ground after a car backfired. Something has you on edge. Fess up."

Jessie looked over at him from the passenger seat and silently debated how forthcoming to be. Ryan was one of only a half dozen people in the world who knew the truth about her family history and her relationship to a never-caught serial killer. He also knew about her father's connection to Bolton Crutchfield, though he wasn't as deeply read in on all the minutiae as Kat Gentry.

It wasn't that she didn't think he could handle it. She just didn't want to burden another person with an update to the nightmare that was her personal history. Still, he deserved to know. If she was going to be working with him a lot, then he might be at risk too. If her father found out where she was, there was no telling who he might hurt to get to her.

"Here's the short version," she said, finally relenting. "Remember how I told you last winter that my father, Xander Thurman, was the Ozarks Executioner?"

"I vaguely recall hearing something about that," Ryan said, a hint of sarcasm in his voice.

"And you recall," she continued, not acknowledging his tone, "that I've been meeting intermittently with Bolton Crutchfield, who viewed my father as a mentor."

"That also strikes a dim bell of recollection."

"And," she pressed on, impressed that he could muster a sense of humor considering the topic, "I mentioned that Crutchfield said my father was looking for me."

Ryan's half-smile disappeared.

"I remember," he said quietly.

"Well, I went to see Crutchfield yesterday and he told me that while I was at Quantico, he somehow spoke to my father again and gave him information about my whereabouts."

"He gave him your address?" Ryan asked incredulously. "He *knows* your address?"

"He was more cryptic than that. He admitted that he didn't know where I live. But he implied that he'd given Xander enough details so that he could find out."

Ryan was quiet for a second.

"When did they have this talk?" he finally asked.

"We're not sure. Kat is going back through the surveillance footage from the last eleven weeks to try and pin that down."

"So your dad could potentially know your exact address by now? Could have known for weeks?"

"It's possible," Jessie admitted. "But I have my doubts that he's figured it out yet. I have pretty robust security measures at my place, some of which were installed by people you recommended. Nothing indicates that they've been breached or that anyone has even tried. I take a circuitous route to access my building. My mail doesn't go there. In theory, he doesn't even know my current name, my job, or what city I live in. I know he found out that I entered Witness Protection years ago. But he may still think I'm living somewhere in Southeast Missouri."

"You don't think Crutchfield gave him any of that?"

"I can't say no for certain," Jessie conceded. "But somehow I don't think so. It's weird to say this. But I don't think he'd consider that very... sporting."

"Okay, so assuming you're right. What happens now?"

"Now, I use caution. I stay on alert. I hope Kat finds something in the footage form NRD. And I lead my life as best I can."

"That's a pretty healthy attitude," Ryan marveled. "You learn that at the FBI?"

"Maybe not *that* specifically. But I did learn not to sweat the things I can't control. I feel physically stronger than I ever have. I've developed investigative skills I didn't have before. I don't feel like I'm faking it... as much. If my father comes for me, I'm about as prepared as I can be. Beyond that, I can't let it consume my life. Although I wouldn't mind having that gun I registered for."

"I'm working on that," Ryan assured her. "The red tape should be cleared up soon."

"That would be great," Jessie said tartly. "Because self-defense classes are nice and all, but a bullet is a solid resource too."

"Update for you. Call me ASAP."

That was all Kat's text had said.

It had come in the middle of the meeting in which Jessie and Ryan were updating Captain Decker on the status of the case. As soon as they left his office, she beelined it to a corner of the station's outdoor courtyard and called back.

"What's up?' she asked as soon as Kat picked up.

"He wasn't lying," her friend answered immediately. "They did meet."

"How did that happen?" Jessie asked in disbelief.

"He disguised himself as a detective from Rampart Division named Joe Capsione, one who had met with Crutchfield previously. He wore a wig and a mustache and what looks like some kind of padding to make him appear heavier. More importantly, he had Capsione's ID."

"Oh god," Jessie muttered.

"Yeah. We've informed his captain and they're sending a team to his apartment now. But obviously, it doesn't bode well. Capsione is single and lives alone and was supposed to be on vacation for a week. No one was looking for him."

"So my father might have planned all this out and waited until the detective's vacation started to maximize his head start."

"It's very likely. He didn't just luck into this."

"When did they meet?" Jessie asked.

"Last Friday," Kat said. "They only talked for about ten minutes."

"What did they say?" Jessie asked.

"I have no idea. Conveniently enough, the meeting took place on the day when the tech guys were doing audio upgrades because of the new cells. So there's no recording of the conversation. I was going to have a friend who can read lips look at it but Cortez pointed out that both men cover their mouths for much of the conversation. So that's a dead end."

"But Crutchfield said they had to talk cryptically because people were listening in," Jessie reminded her. "So why cover their mouths?"

"I'm not sure. It's possible Crutchfield didn't know the audio was out," Kat suggested. "But considering who we're dealing with, I think it's more likely he straight-up lied so we'd have trouble pinpointing when the conversation took place."

"The timing can't be a coincidence, Kat."

"I know. When I'm done with you, I'm going to review the personnel files of everyone from security down to the janitorial staff. I hate to admit it, but we definitely have a mole. What are you going to do?"

"I'm not sure. It's Tuesday now," Jessie said. "So he's had whatever information Crutchfield gave him for over four days. One would think that was enough time to track me down if the info was in any way specific."

"Yeah, but you've only been back in town for about twenty-four hours, Jessie. Maybe he went to your place while you were gone. Even if he sat on it all weekend, he wouldn't have found you."

"I guess," Jessie allowed. "But something makes me think whatever Crutchfield told him was as enigmatic as the clues he gives me. The second he gives up my name or job, he loses all his leverage. Xander Thurman is his hero, but Crutchfield is no sap. He knows that he holds the cards and I don't think he would just lay them all out on the table, even for the Ozarks Executioner."

"You're making a pretty big assumption there," Kat noted.

"I know. But something about what he said to me, about 'home is where the heart is,' makes me think that he's not done playing his little games. I think he wants to give me a fighting chance."

"I hope you're right, Jessie," Kat said skeptically.

"Because your life may depend on it."

CHAPTER EIGHTEEN

In addition to a brutal headache, Jessie's whole body throbbed. She was back at her apartment, finishing up dinner and trying to decompress. But nothing seemed to help. She wasn't sure if it was her extra-intense workout last night or the long, emotionally exhausting day of interrogations, but she felt like she'd been through a meat grinder. She decided to take a few aspirin and a hot shower to soothe her muscles and clean the stink of the case off her.

When she got out, she noticed that she'd missed an hours-old call from her mom. It must have gone straight to voicemail when she was in the Palisades, where cell service was spotty. She played it as she dried off and got dressed.

"Hi, sweetie. It's Ma. Pa told me you called yesterday. Sorry I missed you. I'm so proud of your for passing the FBI thingy. Pa won't tell you this but he's been beaming all day. He told all the guys from the cop crew that he plays poker with. I also want you to know that, despite Pa's joking, I didn't vomit once at dinner last night. Now that I say that out loud, it seems like an odd way to end this message. So how about this? I love you. Talk soon."

Jessie considered calling back, if only to give Ma grief for calling the National Academy program "the FBI thingy."

She glanced at the time. It was 7:30 p.m. here, which meant it was 8:30 in Las Cruces. Under normal circumstances, that wasn't too late to call. But with everything Ma was dealing with physically, she decided to hold off until tomorrow when she was sure she'd be fresher.

She put on sweats, settled in on the couch, and turned on the TV. The shower had helped and the pain medication had kicked in to the point where she only felt mild discomfort now. She stared at the screen as her mind drifted elsewhere.

She actively tried not to think about the meeting between Bolton Crutchfield and her father and what it might have yielded. That path would only lead to a sleepless night.

Instead, she tried to distract herself by focusing on the comparatively cheery topic of Penelope Wooten's murder. As things stood now, she wasn't sure how much progress on the case they'd be able to make in the next day or so.

All three of the primary suspects seemed locked into their stories and unless one of them suddenly confessed, they'd need to wait for the forensic evidence to offer more clues. That wouldn't likely be available until sometime tomorrow. They were in a holding pattern.

Jessie settled in on the couch, trying to imagine Penny's last moments. Based on the defensive wounds on her palms, she had clearly seen the attack coming. How terrifying must it have been to see that large knife coming at her as she realized the threat came from someone she knew, someone she trusted?

Jessie backed up mentally, remembering to employ the tactics she'd learned at the academy and not make assumptions not based on evidence. It was not a certainty that she knew her attacker. While it was unlikely that she would have let a stranger into her home, it wasn't impossible. Or the culprit could have been an acquaintance she knew well enough not to be suspicious of.

She had hit a mental dead end and allowed her thoughts to drift from picturing the kitchen as a crime scene to viewing it a gathering place. It was where the family ate their meals, where the kids did their homework. Would that ever be possible again? How would little Colt Jr. and Anastasia handle learning of their mother's death? What would Colton Wooten say to them?

At first, she suspected he'd want to take them to a hotel for the night. But then she remembered that with Colt's autism, upending his routine could be more damaging than remaining in the residence. It was possible they might have to spend the night in the same house where their own mother had been butchered.

The thought of the place these kids called home being warped into something so horrific was unsettling. She wondered if they'd ever be able to feel comfortable there again. Would Wooten decide they had to move? (That is, assuming he wasn't in prison for their mother's murder.)

Suddenly, a thought, fleeting and distant, bounced around in Jessie's head like a fast-moving pinball. It disappeared before she could latch on to it. She stood up and walked to the kitchen for some water, hoping moving around might help it return.

There it was again, a memory of words more than images, slipping fluidly through her brain, visible but too slippery to fully grasp hold of. She tried to recall what she was thinking about before the flash had come to her. It was something about the kids having to move, having to leave the place they called home. Why were those words so familiar to her?

And then it hit her. Those were the exact words Bolton Crutchfield had used when he told her what he'd revealed to her father.

"I told him the location of the place you call home," he had said after mentioning, seemingly randomly, that "home is where the heart is."

It occurred to her that perhaps Crutchfield hadn't been referring to her current residence. Maybe he was talking about the place that Jessie most considered her home, the place where she'd felt safest and most loved. And if he knew her as well as she feared he did, that could only mean one place: Las Cruces.

CHAPTER NINETEEN

As she got in the taxi, Jessie called Pa for the fourth time.
"LAX," she barked at the cab driver as she listened to the endless ringing. After a minute, she gave up and tried her mom again for what had to be the third or fourth time. When she got no answer, she tried the home phone again. She'd lost track of how many times she'd called that number without success.

She scrolled through her contacts, looking for the management office of the condo complex or one of Pa's retiree buddies. But she couldn't find any and her fingers were shaking. Finally she gave up and just called the Las Cruces FBI field office.

She had to go through a seemingly endless phone tree to reach a live person. When she finally did, she identified herself as being an LAPD profiler rather than a worried daughter and asked for the agent on call. She was immediately transferred.

"Agent Pearsall," a youngish-sounding man said.

"Agent, this is Jessie Hunt. I'm a criminal profiler with the Los Angeles Police Department, Central Station. I'm calling because I'm concerned that a wanted killer I've been tracking has learned the home address of my parents and may want to harm them. One of them is a retired FBI special agent from your office, Bruce Hunt. I've been unable to reach him or my mother, Janice, on any of their phones. I need it checked out ASAP."

She gave the shaky-sounding agent the address, the code to access the building, the location of their hidden front door key, and their interior condo security code.

"Okay, we'll send someone right over," Agent Pearsall assured her.

"Don't send 'someone,' Agent," Jessie said forcefully. "Send everyone. If this killer is there, he's extremely dangerous. He's murdered countless people and evaded capture for over twenty years. You can't just send in one agent or order an officer drive-by. Additionally, these are the parents of someone from another law enforcement agency and one of those at risk is a twenty-five-year FBI veteran. Some professional courtesy is in order. Are we clear?"

"Yes, Ms. Hunt. I'll put out the call as soon as we hang up."

"Thank you. I'm headed to the airport right now. I should be there in a few hours. Don't hesitate to call with updates."

She gave him her number and hung up. She considered calling Ryan Hernandez but decided against it. There was no point in creating anxiety for anyone else just yet. It could be a false alarm, though she knew deep down that it wasn't.

She was given priority boarding on the first flight out of L.A. and was in the air before anyone could call with updates. There were no direct flights to Las Cruces, so she took the first available into El Paso, a forty-five-minute drive away.

She finally landed after 11 p.m. It had been the longest three hours of her life, trapped in a metal tube, uncertain what was going on below her, unable to do anything to help. She tried to pass the time by reading, then by watching a sitcom on the tiny screen in front of her. Nothing helped. Filled with dread, she ended up spending the last two hours of the flight simply staring at the seat-back in front of her.

When she stepped off the Jetway into the terminal, she looked around the near-empty gate area and saw two men in boring suits with safe haircuts standing uncomfortably by the newsstand. She knew they were there for her and walked over.

One was tall and square with brown hair and dark eyes that hinted that he'd seen some difficult things in his life. The other was leaner, with straw-colored hair, freckles, and a nervous manner that suggested he was newer to this sort of thing.

"I'm Jessie Hunt," she said. "I gather you're waiting for me."

"We are," the clearly more experienced of the two said. "I'm Special Agent Miles Gerard and this is Agent Keith Pearsall, who you spoke to earlier. Can you come with us, Ms. Hunt?"

Jessie did as she was asked. Though she was tempted to ask for an update, she held her tongue. Something about the way the men carried themselves told her they had information to share but wanted to do so in a more private environment. That realization filled her with increasing dread.

They arrived at the airport security office. Agent Gerard led the way to a private room at the back that looked like it was likely used for interrogations. When they had all taken seats, he took a deep breath, lifted his head, stared her in the eyes, and began to tell her what she already knew.

"I'm terribly sorry to tell you this, Ms. Hunt. But earlier this evening, we went to your parents' condo and found both of them dead. They had been murdered. We believe it happened earlier this afternoon."

Jessie nodded slightly, gulped hard, and managed to get out a single, clipped sentence.

"Status of the investigation?"

Both men looked surprised by her response. But Gerard rolled with it and answered her question.

"We have investigative and forensic teams onsite now. It looks like your mother was killed first, and quickly. Your father died later. It appears that he was … questioned first."

"Tortured, you mean," Jessie clarified.

"It does appear that he suffered some trauma prior to death, yes."

Jessie nodded. She was about to say something when she felt an onrushing surge of nausea grow within her.

"May I borrow your restroom?" she managed to ask between gritted teeth.

"It's right out the door to the left," Agent Gerard said quickly.

Jessie nodded a second time as she got up and made her way out of the room as fast as she dared. Once in the restroom with the door closed, she took several, long, slow deep breaths, hoping to exhale the queasiness that was causing beads of sweat to form on her forehead.

Flashes of Bruce's and Janine Hunt's faces skirted the edge of her mind, trying to force their way front and center. She gasped involuntarily at the realization that she would never see those faces with smiles on them again. She felt another gasp, something closer to a sob, rising in her chest and battered it back down.

There will be a time for all this. But it's not right now.

She took several more deep breaths until she was sure she was in control, until she was certain she could go back out there and speak to those agents without losing it.

"They had a doorbell security camera, as did most of their neighbors," she said as she reentered the interrogation room, startling both agents. "The whole community is retired law enforcement. The complex has multiple cameras at various entry points. Has all that footage been reviewed yet?"

"We're still going through it," Agent Gerard said, not commenting on her brief absence. "But the initial review suggests the suspect used a laser device to blind the cameras he was aware of. We're still hopeful that he might have missed some and we can get a few images. We haven't been able to access your parents' personal footage yet."

"I can give you the code for that. Take me there, please. The sooner we're onsite, the less the scene will have been compromised and the more accurate a picture I can get of what happened."

The agents stared silently at her for a second. To her surprise, it was Pearsall who spoke up first.

"With all due respect, Ms. Hunt," he said, "it's a pretty grisly scene right now. You might want to wait until CSU has had an opportunity to clean up a bit."

Jessie stood up and looked at both men with cold certainty.

"Take me there now."

CHAPTER TWENTY

As Jessie approached the wreckage of what had been her parents' "home sweet home," she forced herself to remember her training. If there was ever a situation in which she'd need to depend on it, this was it.

Follow the evidence. Let it tell the story of what happened here. Don't try to shoehorn it into an existing theory. Don't jump to conclusions. Don't let it get personal.

That last one was going to be hard.

She stood outside the front door for a few seconds, willing her mind to become a blank slate so that she could absorb the scene she was about to observe without emotion or prejudice. She knew it was an almost impossible task. But if she was going to get justice for Bruce and Janine Hunt—her true parents—she would have to set aside her own feelings for as long as she could.

She snapped on her forensic gloves, put baggy plastic slippers over her shoes, took several deep breaths, and walked through the front door. The first thing she noticed was that there were two teams working what appeared to be separate crime scenes.

She walked down the hall to where the smaller group was assembled, in her parents' bedroom. Agents Gerard and Pearsall followed from a respectful distance, ready to answer any questions she might have.

She entered the bedroom and saw Janine Hunt lying on the bed. She was in sweatpants and a long-sleeved cotton shirt she'd gotten in Cancun a few years ago. It read "Margarita is my middle name. No, really."

Her eyes were open and her head was turned unnaturally to the left, a result of her neck having been snapped. Jessie looked away for a second, blinked a few times, took a moment to regroup, and then returned her gaze to the bed.

Other than the injury that killed her, Ma looked generally undisturbed. Her thin brown hair, patchy in parts, was exposed and her wig rested on the bedside table. The creases at the edges of her eyes seemed somehow less pronounced now.

Either she had not been aware of what was about to happen to her or Xander Thurman had adjusted her body to look peaceful after he'd killed her. Her arms rested loosely at her sides. She had on thick socks, as her feet always got cold and tingly in the days after chemo.

Jesse let her eyes wander around the room, looking for anything out of the ordinary. There was nothing. The closet door was closed. The bathroom door was slightly ajar. The TV was off and the remote rested on top of it. The old-fashioned VCR was to the right. The display panel, which read "play," was so covered in dust that the word was barely visible. No family photos seemed to have been taken. It looked normal, apart from the murdered woman on the bed.

Jessie stepped out and walked down the hall to where the large group of investigators had congregated in the den. When she got closer, she saw what was of such interest. It occurred to her that her mother had gotten off easy. She knelt down, pretending to tie her shoe, even though it was covered in a slipper. While on one knee, she allowed herself to silently exhale the cry that had materialized in her lungs. The image before her was brutally, painfully familiar.

Bruce Hunt was seated in a dining room chair, his forearms taped to the wooden armrests. His legs were tied to the legs of the chair. His eyelids were taped wide open. And there was a long, deep knife cut across his chest from his left shoulder to just below his neck.

Jessie's hand involuntarily went up to the spot on her chest where she had a scar that matched his wound exactly, just as everything else about the scene did. When Xander had forced little Jessica Thurman to watch him kill her mother, he had tied her arms and legs to a chair and taped her eyes open. He'd sliced a long gash along her upper chest too. It was all the same, with one exception.

Her father had a second knife wound in his chest. The weapon was nowhere in sight but it must have been big because the hole in the flesh over his heart was about as big around as a golf ball. Blood, now mostly dried, had dribbled down his front and rested in a puddle between his feet.

He looked so fragile. His burly chest was curled in on itself. His previously sinewy arms sagged. He was no longer the man she both respected and occasionally resented, who'd kept her safe from harm all those years. He was just an old man, pushed to the breaking point before being killed.

Pushing the onrushing wave of grief off to the side, Jessie forced herself to look around the den, hunting for anything unusual, anything significantly different from her visit less than three months prior. Nothing jumped out at her but she didn't trust her powers of observation at this exact moment.

"Make sure they take lots of pictures of the room," she muttered, speaking to Gerard and Pearsall for the first time since entering the apartment. "I'll want to study the details more closely later."

They both nodded as Jessie stepped back outside into the cool, late-night New Mexico air. She walked several steps away and sat down on a bench near a small, path-side garden. Her mind was swimming.

This had all been done for her—either as punishment or warning. It was a reminder of what Xander had once done many years ago to the person she loved most in the world. It was a reminder that he could still get to the people she cared about, the people who made her feel safe.

In a weird way that she couldn't quite explain and didn't want to think about, this was also his way of reintroducing himself to her after so many years away. He was saying "I'm back."

❧ ❧ ❧

Jessie sat outside the apartment for another hour while the assorted teams did their work, processing evidence and then removing her adoptive parents' bodies. Eventually Gerard walked over.

"We'll want you to come to the medical examiner's office to officially sign off on the identifications," he said quietly. "They'll need to hold on to the bodies for a few days for the investigation. But they should be able to release them to you by the end of the week, the weekend at the latest."

"Thanks," she said, not looking up.

"John Brode, the agent in charge for our office, was hoping to talk to you tonight or tomorrow. He wanted to get whatever you could give him on your suspect."

"I'll give him a statement tonight. Can he meet us at the M.E.'s office?"

"Sure, I'll tell him," Gerard promised. "Do you have a place to stay? I can make a few recommendations if you like."

"That's okay. Once we get everything squared away tonight, I plan to go straight back to L.A. I'll take your lodging recommendations for when I come back for the funeral, maybe this weekend."

"You're leaving town tomorrow?" he asked incredulously.

"Yeah, I'm in the middle of a case. Besides, I have a feeling the guy who did this is headed there next. This was just an opening act for him."

Her phone pinged. Turning away from the open-mouthed FBI agent, she looked at the message and gasped. It was from her pa, Bruce Hunt.

CHAPTER TWENTY-ONE

It took Jessie a few seconds to figure out what must have happened. The message wasn't, as she'd hoped, some declaration of love from beyond the grave. Instead it was simply a confirmation that an Amazon order he'd placed had been processed. The order, to be delivered to Jessie, was for the compact disc of an album called *The Best of Bobby McFerrin.*

She looked at the time the order had been placed—4:17 p.m.—and realized that it was right in the window when he was being tortured. It occurred to her that he must have placed the order through their Alexa device while he was strapped down in the chair. And since it was being sent to her, it was almost certainly intended as some kind of coded message for her.

She clicked on the link for the album and scrolled down to the track listing, hoping to uncover whatever that message might be. She only vaguely recalled the name Bobby McFerrin and couldn't immediately think of any songs by him.

The she saw it. The first song on the album was one she was familiar with, though she'd never known who sang it. It was called "Don't Worry Be Happy."

A flood of memories suddenly overwhelmed her. This was the song Pa had most often sung to her as a lullaby when she was a child. He sang it in the first months after she came to live with them, when she was still shell-shocked over what happened and couldn't get to sleep. He sang it when she woke up screaming in the middle of the night. And it helped.

She recalled that, at a certain point, all he had to do was hum a few bars of it to calm her down. He did it just before she skied down her first intermediate slope, just before she went onstage in the elementary school play, and just before he popped her dislocated finger back into place during softball practice.

It had a Pavlovian ability to calm her. It was his way of saying "I'm here and everything's going to be okay." But in this case, Jessie suddenly understood, it meant something slightly different. It meant "I will protect you." It was his way of letting her know that no matter what torture was inflicted on him, Bruce Hunt was not going to reveal anything about her life or location.

Jessie loved Pa for that. She loved how, even in his moment of greatest pain, he had still been as Bruce Hunt as ever. He'd kept his wits about him. He had come up with a plan. He'd done everything he could to protect his little girl.

But she knew it had been a futile gesture. Pa couldn't keep her safe from Xander Thurman. At best he'd delayed the inevitable. Now equipped with her new name and having seen the photos of her displayed throughout the condo, the Ozarks Executioner would eventually find her.

As she stared blankly at her phone screen, another thought occurred to Jessie. She glanced over at Gerard and Pearsall, who were standing off to the side, both eyeing her apprehensively.

"Any reason I can't go back in the condo?" she asked.

Gerard shook his head.

"The scene has been processed," he assured her. "You're good."

She walked back in and surveyed the living room. The chair Pa had been strapped to was a good fifteen feet from the Alexa device, which sat on the breakfast bar between the living room and kitchen. To have ensured his CD order was heard, he would have had to have spoken loudly. It was hard to imagine that Xander would have allowed him to do that. That meant that he must have placed the order when Xander was elsewhere.

Where in the condo would Xander have gone for long enough that Bruce would have felt confident placing the order?

It would have had to be far enough away that Bruce felt certain he wouldn't be overheard. Jessie walked back down the hall, trying to recreate the movements Xander likely would have taken. She glanced at the guest bathroom, acknowledging that it was possible he'd gone in there, allowing Bruce time to place the order. But somehow that didn't feel right.

She stepped back into her parents' bedroom. The bed was now empty and stripped of sheets. Just about everything else was as it had been before. But she had a feeling, not based on any forensic analysis, that this was where Xander had been when Bruce placed the order. And he was doing something in here that made Bruce sure he could order the CD without being heard. An ugly thought popped into her head.

"My mother wasn't sexually assaulted, correct?" she asked Gerard, who was lingering halfway down the hall.

"No," he said. "They'll do a full workup at the medical examiner's. But there was no initial indication of any trauma other than the injury to her neck."

Jessie nodded and returned her attention to the bedroom, letting her eyes casually scan it. Just as before, nothing seemed out of place. Her eyes rested on the television.

Almost nothing.

She saw the remote control, sitting on top of the set, and realized: there was no justification for the remote to be there. In her weakened state, Ma would have kept the remote beside the bed. Pa would have had no reason to move it. Even if he was using it, he'd have left it on his side of the bed. There was no reason to put it on the television.

Xander had moved it.

Why?

She moved closer to the screen, then glanced over at the VCR and registered something that had escaped her notice when she'd been in here before. Her parents were no tech wizards, as evidenced by the fact that they still had a VCR at all. And for as long as she could remember, it always flashed that familiar "12:00" on the screen.

But now, under a thick layer of dust, the display read "play." That meant that someone had put a videotape in the machine. It was waiting to be watched.

She glanced back over her shoulder to make sure neither FBI agent had entered the room. Then she pushed the eject button. A video cassette emerged from the slot. One look at it confirmed her suspicions that it was from Xander.

Taped to the spine of the cassette was a small Post-it with one word handwritten in black ink: JUNEBUG.

That was her father's pet name for her when she was a little girl. The tape was intended for her. Without thinking, she removed it from the machine and slid it into her jacket pocket.

"Let's go," she called out to the agents in the hall. "There's nothing here."

CHAPTER TWENTY-TWO

Jessie had to remind herself that she was not in any immediate danger.

As she stood outside the terminal at the L.A. airport, waiting for Kat Gentry to pick her up, she told herself that her father would not want to cut her up, at least not until he was sure she'd viewed whatever was on that tape. Until she'd seen the message, she was almost certainly safe.

Jessie looked at her watch. It was 10:51 a.m. She had been in Las Cruces less than twelve hours. After formally identifying her parents' bodies at the medical examiner's and giving Special Agent in Charge Brode a detailed but intentionally incomplete description of who the Ozarks Executioner was, she booked a flight back to Los Angeles and asked Agent Pearsall to give her a ride.

She promised to return over the weekend for the funeral and answer any additional questions they might have. There was no reason for her to stay in Las Cruces and several to get back to L.A. She needed to warn the folks at Central Station that there was a dangerous serial killer on the loose. She needed to confront Bolton Crutchfield about what had happened. And she needed to find a quiet place to watch the video Xander had left for her.

As Kat pulled up to the curb and waved to her, Jessie felt a sudden pang of emotion at the sight of her. After an entire night of remaining steely and professional, she finally saw a friendly face. She knew her system was desperate to let down its guard, to genuinely feel the impact of the events from last night. But she couldn't do that just yet. So she forced the feeling back down.

Kat got out and walked around the car, extending her arms to wrap Jessie in an embrace.

"I'm so sorry," she whispered as she squeezed her tight.

"Thanks," Jessie said, impressed at how measured her own voice sounded. "Let's get out of here."

Thankfully, Kat didn't pepper her with questions on the ride to the station, which was mostly silent. Jessie had filled her in when she'd called from the El Paso airport to ask for the ride. She'd also asked Kat to get in touch with Ryan Hernandez to update him. She didn't feel up to repeating the same story multiple times.

"Ryan said that Captain Decker has blocked off meeting time for you when we arrive. He gave him the basics, though you'll probably have to fill in the gaps."

"I don't relish that," Jessie admitted. "He's going to want to know why I wasn't more forthcoming earlier."

"You have no obligation on that front," Kat insisted. "Up until now, we didn't know if Crutchfield was all talk. We didn't know what your father was planning. There was nothing to tell."

"I don't know that he'll see it that way."

"Jessie, I'd be surprised if he reads you the riot act under the circumstances. He knows you've … been through a lot. How are you holding up by the way? Have you slept?"

"I got a few hours on the flight," Jessie said. "Otherwise, I've mostly sealed off how I feel from the facts of what happened."

"Is that healthy?" Kat asked.

"Probably not," Jessie admitted. "But if I let myself start reminiscing or grieving, I'm going to fall apart. And I can't let that happen right now. Xander is still out there and he has some kind of larger plan I don't get yet. I need to keep focused and resolved so I can get him. My folks' funeral is this weekend. I'll work through my feelings for them then. But for now, I can't let down my guard."

"May I come to the funeral?" Kat asked quietly.

"That would be nice," Jessie said.

They both ignored the catch in her throat.

❧ ❧ ❧

The bullpen got noticeably quiet when they walked in. Jessie pretended not to notice and walked over to her desk with Kat right behind her. Ryan saw her coming and stood up. When she arrived, he gave her a quick hug.

"Let me know if there's anything I can do," he said quietly in her ear. "If you need a sounding board, a chauffeur, a delivery person, or a punching bag, I'm here."

"Thanks, Ryan," she said. "For now, what I need to do is to catch the man who did this. Everything thing else is secondary."

"Understood. Let's go talk to the captain and see how we can make that happen."

They started for his office when Ryan looked back and saw Kat standing by Jessie's desk.

"You should come too," he said. "Considering your line of work, it's possible that you might have some information that could help."

Kat nodded and they all walked into Captain Decker's office. He was on the phone but waved them to the large couch against the far wall. He got off just as they sat down and stood up awkwardly. He didn't walk over to her but he did nod sympathetically.

"Hernandez gave me an update on what happened, Hunt. I'm truly sorry for your loss."

"Thank you, Captain."

"Know that the department is here to support you in every way possible. You have full access to mental health resources, including a grief counselor. We have generous bereavement time in the benefits plan. There are support groups available. We're all here for you."

"I appreciate it, Captain," Jessie reiterated.

"Okay, this is the hard part. I'm sure you're exhausted and I don't want to overwhelm you. As I said, Hernandez filled me in a bit. And I don't need you to go over what happened in New Mexico. But I was hoping you could flesh out your connection to this Thurman guy. I know there is one but it's all a bit fuzzy to me. It needs to be much clearer if we're going to keep you safe."

Jessie looked over at Ryan, surprised.

"I didn't get into the personal stuff," he said quietly. "I didn't think it was my place."

She nodded. Part of her appreciated his discretion. But at this moment, she almost wished he'd already spilled everything so she didn't have to.

"It's kind of a long story," she said.

"I've got time," Captain Decker assured her.

So she told him everything. She started with her youth in Southeast Missouri and how her real name was Jessica Thurman. She moved on to her father abducting her and her mother, taking them to an isolated cabin in the Ozarks and once they arrived, revealing that he'd been killing people there for years. She shared how he murdered her mother while she watched and then left her for dead.

She ignored his eyes getting wider when she informed him that her father subsequently got the moniker the Ozarks Executioner and dropped off the grid entirely. She talked about how she was put in Witness Protection and placed with a New Mexico FBI agent and his wife. She talked about how, after that, she'd led what looked on paper to be a reasonably normal life as Jessie Hunt. That is, until her own husband tried to kill her.

Finally, with some input from Kat, she filled him in on how she'd learned that her father had been in contact with Bolton Crutchfield and how, despite being locked up, Crutchfield had somehow managed to pass information about Jessie's adoptive family to him.

"You know the rest," she concluded.

Decker sat quietly in his chair for a solid minute before responding. Jessie could tell he wanted to broach the fact that she'd kept all of this to herself until now. But to his credit, he steered clear of that topic. Instead, he addressed his first question to Kat.

"Are you able to screen grab images of Thurman so we can distribute them?"

"Unfortunately, the second time he visited Crutchfield, he was in an elaborate disguise as a detective from Rampart Division whose body was discovered bludgeoned and left in his bathtub yesterday. The first visit from two years ago might be more helpful. He was still disguised but it was less detailed, probably because we didn't know to look for him at that point. What do you think, Jessie?"

"Yes, the first visit, when he assumed the identity of a psychology professor, looked a fair bit like how I suspect he'd appear now."

"Okay," Decker said. "Then we'll go off that, maybe have our tech folks digitally alter him so that we have several variations to work from. That's a start at least. In the meantime, we're going to give you a protective detail, Hunt."

"What? Why?"

"You're kidding, right?" he said, incredulous. "This guy murdered your parents and it looks like he's after you next. Don't you think we should take a few precautions?"

"I'm not sure what he wants."

"I'm not sure it matters," he countered. "There's a serial killer on the loose. And if he doesn't know your location yet, he will soon. We need to prepare for that eventuality."

"But I need to be able to move freely to work," she protested. "I want to go see Crutchfield. He's the reason this happened. I want to look him in the eye and confront him."

"Are you sure that's the best move under the circumstances?" Decker asked, dubious.

"It's actually not a bad idea," Kat piped in. "Crutchfield has some kind of thing for Jessie. It's hard to explain. I wouldn't call it a crush as much as…admiration. Thurman is his mentor and I think he originally planned to do the bidding of the serial killer he modeled himself after. But once he met Jessie, he started to like her. He started to respect her. He's developed a strange affection for her. I think his loyalties are conflicted. If she goes into his cell and challenges him about his culpability in the Hunts' deaths, it might have some impact."

"You think he's going to feel remorseful?" Decker asked, disbelieving.

"No," Kat said. "He's a serial killer. He doesn't do remorse. But he does view himself as a practitioner of fair play. He may feel that since he gave Thurman information that led to the Hunts dying, he owes Jessie something in return, if only to be sporting."

"That does sound like him," Jessie agreed. "If we can appeal to his warped sense of honor, he might offer up something useful."

Decker still looked skeptical but ultimately shrugged.

"Frankly, I'm open to just about anything at this point. We're in a tough spot."

"Then we'll head out to Norwalk now," Jessie said.

"Fine. But after that, you're on official leave. I want you to go home and get some rest. You look terrible. And I'm assigning you that protective detail. They'll be joining you for your trip to see Crutchfield and escorting you home, where they will remain until further notice."

Jessie was about to protest when she saw Ryan shake his head imperceptibly. Despite her misgivings, she bit her tongue and nodded. With the meeting over, they began to file out.

"Do we have any old VCRs in this place?" she asked Ryan as they left Decker's office. "I don't have one and I was hoping there was a machine I could borrow."

"Sure. They have a bunch of old unclaimed ones near the evidence room. Why?"

"I found an old video at my folks' place. I was hoping to look at it later. It might have some footage of better times with my family. I could use that, you know?"

"I get it," he said. "Why don't you go do your bereavement leave paperwork? It won't take long. In the meantime, I'll snag a VCR for you."

"Thanks, Ryan," she said.

As she watched him go, she felt a small pang of guilt at her deception. But it faded quickly when she remembered why she had done it. The Ozarks Executioner had a private message for her. And she needed to watch it—soon.

Chapter Twenty Three

When they got to NRD, Jessie and Kat left the protective detail behind.

The two men Captain Decker had assigned, Officers Beatty and Nettles, had followed them to Norwalk in a black-and-white. Beatty, blond-haired and gangly, was an enthusiastic rookie. He'd made a few mistakes when dealing with a suspect in a previous case Jessie handled, but he was diligent and high energy. It was unlikely that he'd drift off while guarding her apartment.

Nettles, older, burlier, and more grizzled, had flecks of gray in his black hair. Jessie had never worked with him before. But Ryan told her that he was a total pro who could be a hard ass when he needed to. Ryan also warned her that he had a wife and two young kids at home so he probably wouldn't be over the moon about this assignment. His taciturn demeanor when they were introduced bore that out.

The two officers were allowed to loiter in the small waiting area by the front desk of the NRD facility. But once Kat took Jessie into Transitional Prep, they remained behind.

"You don't have security authorization," Kat had told them, ending the matter.

They went through the security routine quickly and made it into the lockdown unit in less than ten minutes. When Kat opened the door, Ernie Cortez glanced over.

The second he saw Jessie, he walked toward her. There was none of his flirty bravado now. He simply wrapped his massive arms around her and squeezed. When he released her, his eyes were damp. He looked like he wanted to say something but couldn't find the words.

"Thanks, Ernie," Jessie said, letting him off the hook.

He nodded, and with a sniffle returned to his post. Jessie glanced over at Kat, who smiled slightly and shrugged.

Two minutes later, Jessie walked into Bolton Crutchfield's cell. She had the emergency key fob in her left hand, though she was determined not to use it. Crutchfield was lying on his back on his metal-framed bed, reading a battered, dog-eared paperback. When Jessie and Kat entered, he sat up, a mildly surprised expression on his face.

"To what do I owe the hono—" he began before Jessie cut him off.

"They're dead," she said sharply. "Bruce and Janine Hunt are dead."

Crutchfield delicately placed the paperback on the mattress, then looked up, meeting Jessie's eyes.

"That is unexpected," he said slowly.

"You told my father where to find them and you figured he'd just want to chat?" Jessie demanded incredulously.

Crutchfield didn't speak for a few seconds. When he finally did, his voice was hushed.

"First, I didn't tell him where to find them. I gave him a clue, which I assumed, if he was able to use it, would lead him to your former home. I thought he might deduce your current whereabouts based on that information. Second, I thought it likely that he would want to keep a low profile, gather the necessary details to find you, and depart without making his presence known. In retrospect, I see that I erred in that assumption."

"Ya think?"

"Clearly," he continued, ignoring her sarcasm, "I didn't properly consider the level of animosity your father would have toward the people he viewed as usurping his parenting role. I also apparently overestimated his concern about getting caught."

"Yeah, you seem to have made a lot of errors in judgment," Jessie agreed venomously. "And now two innocent people are dead as a result."

"I regret that," he said flatly.

Jessie took a long, slow, deep breath, forcing herself to remain calm. As upset as she was, it served no purpose to scream and shout at him. She needed whatever information he could offer and attacking him, however satisfying, would surely be counterproductive.

"Maybe there's a way to mitigate the damage you've done," she finally said.

"It seems that ship has sailed, Miss Jessie."

"For my parents, yes," she agreed, keeping her voice even. "But Xander Thurman is still out there. He's looking for me. And it's quite clear that he has ill intent. Unless it's your wish that he succeed, help me. Otherwise it's very possible that this will be the last time we speak. I may not be around much longer."

"How can I possibly help you?" he asked. "I'm incarcerated."

"You've met with him twice recently. You know how he thinks. Give me some tools so that I can protect myself. You owe me that," she implored.

"I'm afraid that your father was very cagey with me. He knew that I was enthused to be in his presence and that I would consider that enough of a thrill to help him, even if there was nothing of consequence in it for me."

"He must have given you some sense of why he was looking for me," Jessie insisted.

"Nothing specific, unfortunately. I think his trust in me only went so far."

Jessie sat there at the desk across from his glass-walled cell, quietly thinking. For the first time in their interaction together, she didn't get the impression that Crutchfield was playing her. He seemed to genuinely not know what her father intended.

"There was one thing," he finally conceded. "I hesitate to even mention it because I'm not sure it's of any significance. But if it helps you better understand how your father's mind works, perhaps it will be of assistance. He kept talking about family."

"What do you mean?"

"He said he wanted to reunite you with the family. He wanted the family to be together. I didn't know if that was intended as a metaphor, as in he would kill you and reunite you with your dead mother. Or if it was intended as a literal desire—to kidnap you and take you to some island populated solely by members of the Thurman clan. But it seemed important to him. Did he make a big fuss about family when you were a child?"

"No," Jessie recalled. "I met a few relatives on my mom's side when we'd visit. I don't even remember where they lived but it wasn't near us. I don't think I ever met a single member of my father's family."

"Then it does seem odd that it would be of such consequence to him now," Crutchfield mused. "Don't you agree?"

Jessie stared at him through narrowed eyes.

"How do I know this is legit and that you're not just screwing with me?"

Crutchfield looked mildly offended.

"I suppose you don't," he admitted. "I can't prove that what I say is true. All I can do is tell you what he said. You can choose whether to believe me or not. I'm not even sure how it might be of use to you. But it's all I have to offer."

Jessie didn't know why, but she did believe him. Still, she stood up and pushed the chair back, ready to leave. To her surprise, Crutchfield stood up as well and walked over so that he was right in front of the glass divider, only five feet from her.

"Miss Jessie," he said quietly, "you are familiar with my crimes. I cannot pretend that I am capable of the kind of empathy one might expect in this situation. But I can tell you that in the time we have come to know each other, I have developed a reluctant respect for you. Testing wits against you has been invigorating. I hope you believe that it was never my wish that those you care for pay the price they have. It would not have been my choice."

"Is this an apology?" Jessie asked.

"It's an acknowledgment of my shortcomings. And should your father find you and slice you into ribbons, I will be glad to have said it."

"Thanks," Jessie said sarcastically, turning for the door.

"One more thing, Miss Jessie," Crutchfield called out. "You are almost free."

"What?"

"You won't want to hear this but you should view yourself much as an involuntary psychiatric patient strapped to a table. Your New Mexico family was tying you down. They were a source of authority, one which bound you to traditional perceptions of morality. Their deaths, however painful for you, have partially unbound you from those strictures. Now only your father remains. He binds you to some sense of loyalty to the past. Once you have broken loose from the hold he still has on you, you will finally be unshackled, free to pursue your true mission, no longer haunted by the authority figures who have defined your life until now."

Jessie stared at him open-mouthed, stunned at the bounty of madness he'd just verbally vomited.

"You know," she finally replied, "sometimes, with your gentlemanly drawl and polite demeanor, I forget."

"Forget what?" Crutchfield asked, his eyes blazing with righteous intensity.

"That you're bat-shit crazy."

Then, without another word, she turned and left.

Chapter Twenty Four

Jessie stared at the TV monitor, her finger hovering over the VCR "play" button, debating whether to push it.

She was in the bedroom of her apartment, truly alone for the first time in twenty-four hours. She and Kat had parted ways at NRD and Officers Beatty and Nettles had escorted her back to the city. Jessie had convinced them to abandon their black-and-white, check out a less conspicuous vehicle, and change into plain clothes.

"The goal is to avoid attention, not draw it," she'd told them.

So after they'd done that, the three of them made a grocery run and went back to her apartment. She showed them her round-about "lose a tail" route through the adjacent retail complex, which Nettles seemed to get but Beatty looked perplexed by.

When they got to the lobby of the condo building, Nettles went to talk to Fred the security guard while Beatty went upstairs with her. While he checked out her various security measures, she threw a frozen pizza in the oven for the three of them. A few minutes later, Nettles joined them and filled them in.

"I told your security guard buddy Fred that I was assisting a resident who had filed a restraining order against an ex. I wasn't specific about who and he didn't ask me for details. He knows to call my cell if he sees anyone suspicious."

After pizza and a few *Top Chef* reruns, Jessie told them she was exhausted and was calling it a night. She gave them some blankets and pillows and left them to work out their sleeping accommodations. There was only one couch and she suspected Beatty, the junior officer, would be spending the night on the floor.

She took a shower, changed into sweats, locked the bedroom door, and walked over to the VCR she'd set up earlier. She could hear that the guys had changed the channel to some Jason Statham action movie and knew that it was loud enough to cover the volume of whatever she was about to watch.

Finally, annoyed at her own hesitance, she stopped lingering over the "play" button and pushed it. The screen went from blue to static and then finally to a shot of what she recognized as her parents' bedroom.

The image remained unchanged for several seconds, long enough for Jessie to think it might be frozen. But then a man stepped into the frame. He was much as she remembered him from the prison video and from her childhood. Tall and lean, his arms ropy strong, and he had catcher's mitt–sized hands.

He wore a black ski mask over his face so that only his eyes and mouth were visible. She thought she saw facial hair around his lips but couldn't be certain in the poorly lit room. His eyes, the same green hue as her own, were also the same as in her nightmares— cold and penetrating.

In the two-year-old prison video with Crutchfield, his black hair had been graying. But with the mask, she didn't know if that had advanced or if he'd possibly shaved it off altogether. The fact that he was hiding his face suggested he made alterations he didn't want her to be aware of. He confirmed as much with his first words; the first time she'd heard his voice since she was six.

"Sorry for the cloak and dagger stuff, Junebug," he said, pointing to the mask. "I just want you to be surprised when we meet up. Can't have that if you know what's coming, right?"

His voice was low and gravelly, like someone had taken sandpaper to his vocal cords.

Was that how he always sounded? Or did I just block it out all these years?

"By the time you see this, the nice folks who live here will be cold. Part of me regrets that. I tried to get Brucie to tell me a bit about what you were like growing up since I missed out on so much.

But he's not being real hospitable; real closed-mouthed, that one. I imagine that'll change a bit when I introduce him to the blade. Doesn't matter that much anyway. We can catch up more in person soon. That's what I really wanted to talk to you about, Junebug."

He adjusted the mask, which had moved slightly to cover his mouth, then resumed talking.

"I've been looking for you a long time, Jessica. Our family has been apart for far too long. But I'm going to remedy that real soon. That Bolton was a real tease, refusing to give me your current particulars. But I've been looking around the place here and even though your replacement parents kept almost no paperwork on you, I gleaned a few details."

He smiled through the mask, clearly enjoying the drama of the moment.

"Now that I know you are Jessie Hunt and that you're a forensic profiler, it won't take me long to find out where you're hanging your hat these days. And when I do, you're going to have a decision to make."

He stopped talking for a second and stepped out of frame. When he returned, he was wiping his mouth as if he'd just had a sip of something. Oddly, he seemed slightly nervous, as if he were stalling in saying the next part.

"Here's the deal, Junebug. Your training was cut short. When I came back to the cabin to get you all those years ago, you were gone. You can't imagine how disappointed I was, all that effort for nothing. But now we're going to get a chance to pick up where we left off. You see, I was upset at first when I heard your new name was Hunt. But now I know it was meant to be because we are going on a hunt together, Junebug. It's time for you to reclaim your family's legacy.

"We are going to get back in the business of taking the lives of the unrighteous, only now we'll do it together. There are far too many unworthy souls out there. It's the Thurman family's duty to thin the herd. And it's time you stepped up."

There was knock on the bedroom door. Jessie jumped slightly and hit "pause."

"Yeah?" she called out.

"Just heard voices in there and wanted make sure you were okay," Nettles said from the other side of the door.

"I'm cool," she answered quickly. "Just watching a little TV before I crash for the night."

"Okay," he said through the door. "We'll turn the volume down out here. Let us know if you need anything, all right?"

"I will," Jessie assured him. "Thanks, Officer Nettles."

"No problem," he said and she heard footsteps as he retreated from the door.

To be safe, she turned the volume down and moved closer to the television monitor before hitting "play" again. Her father's stationary image clicked back into motion.

"We both know the real reason you became a profiler, Junebug," he said softly. "It's in your blood, girl. You've got the same instincts as your daddy. You've got a taste for the killing. And you hoped that by hunting down these killers, you could immerse yourself in their worlds without becoming one of them. It's like getting a contact high.

"But you know as well as I do, it's not enough. Once you get a taste for it, you can't just nibble. You have to take a big bite. It's time to chomp down, Junebug. It's time to accept your true nature and cross over."

Jessie squirmed involuntarily as she stood in place. It was as if Xander had reached into her brain and activated a part of it she'd forcibly kept dormant for years. All her anxieties about whether the child of someone who lived to kill inherited that instinct rose up inside her. She physically gulped, as if that would contain her unease.

"So here's what's going to happen," he continued cheerily. "You have a choice, darlin'. You can accept your birthright and join the family quest. Or you can become the first sacrifice on the altar of the new world we're creating here. You see, the way I look at it, if you're not willing to join up and make the family proud, there's no point in letting you take up space. You're either part of the problem or part of the solution, Junebug. And if you choose to be a problem, then I'm here to be your solution.

"So this is my proposal. I'm taping this video on Tuesday afternoon. I figure that by sometime this evening, these nice people here will be found and you'll be contacted. So let's call it a loose forty-eight hours. I expect that you'll reach out to me by Thursday evening, let's say around eight p.m. If you look at the other side of the Post-it on the videotape with your name on it, I've included an e-mail address. You can get hold of me through that."

Jessie made a mental note to have the tech team learn everything about the e-mail address and see if it could offer any leads.

"One more thing, kiddo," he added, seemingly reading her mind. "Follow my instructions and you'll be fine. Disobey them and…not so much. I know you're a smart girl but don't get too smart. I may not be a spring chicken but I've learned a thing or two about how the interwebs work. If you try to play me or get a jump on me by following my digital footprint or setting up some kind of sting, I'll know. And I will not be amused. There will be consequences for those who assist you. Just ask Mr. and Mrs. Hunt how it goes for people who get between me and my progeny. You've been warned."

Jessie didn't know if he was bluffing or not. But the idea of putting her co-workers at risk to save her own skin was something she didn't think she could handle. Her father moved on, oblivious to her internal conflict.

"I'm real hopeful that you'll make the right choice here, Junebug. If you do, we can accomplish incredible things together. If you don't, well, you remember how things went for your mama. Talk to you soon."

He stepped out of frame again and a moment later the screen cut to black. Jessie sat on the end of her bed, trying to wrap her ahead around everything her father had said. It was simply too much. She felt as if her brain was bubbling over.

For the time being, as a way to short-circuit the panic she felt beginning to overtake her, she set aside his claims about her "true

nature" and focused on the more immediate concern—the count-
down he'd established for her. She looked at her bedside clock.
It was just after 9 p.m. on Wednesday night. That meant that she
had just under twenty-four hours until he expected some kind of
response.

And as he viewed it, she had only two choices: join him in a
murder spree or be its first victim.

CHAPTER TWENTY FIVE

There was one positive element to Xander's ultimatum. It meant Jessie was safe until his deadline, which meant that she could go to sleep without fearing that he would break into her apartment and kill everyone there. The second she came to that realization, she fell into a deep slumber that she didn't awaken from until Officer Beatty knocked on her door the next morning.

"You okay in there?" he called out.

She looked groggily over at the clock. It was 7:04 a.m. She'd slept for almost ten hours, uninterrupted.

"I'm good," she shouted back. "I'll be out in a couple of minutes."

After a quick freshening up, she stepped into her living room where she found both officers fully dressed and sipping coffee.

"Nettles made you some eggs," Beatty said, nodding at the plate on the counter. "His wife says it's the only thing he can't ruin."

"Shut it, Beatty," Nettles said. "That was shared in confidence. Remind me never to recommend you for an undercover assignment."

"Thanks," she said, ignoring their squabbling as she shuffled over. "You guys sleep okay?'

"We slept," Nettles said noncommittally. "What about you?"

"Surprisingly well," she admitted. "I had a thought last night that calmed me down a bit."

"What's that?" Beatty asked.

"I don't know how much the captain read you guys in. But my father—you know, the notorious serial killer ..."

"We're aware," Nettles said drily.

"Well, he told another serial killer he's been in contact with that he wants our family to be reunited again."

"How did that calm you down?" Beatty asked. "That would freak me out."

"He didn't say he wanted to butcher me," she noted, careful to only share the bare minimum necessary to make her point. "He said he wanted to reunite. That distinction was enough to help me relax a bit. And that's all it took for me to crash hard."

"Whatever works, I guess," Nettles said, clearly not convinced. "So what do we have on the agenda for today? Because I was thinking it couldn't hurt to get this building a few additional exterior cameras; maybe place them across the street."

"Actually I had a different plan," Jessie told him. "I was thinking of going in to work today."

Though she knew she shouldn't have, Jessie got enormous pleasure from watching both officers' jaws drop wide open.

She got the same endorphin rush an hour later.

That was when she repeated her request to Captain Decker in his office and got a similar slack-jawed reaction.

"You want to do what?" he demanded as Ryan shifted uncomfortably on the couch beside her.

"Look," she said calmly. "I can't just hole up in my apartment for days on end. I'll go stir-crazy. Besides, I'm a sitting duck there, just waiting for him to show up."

"I thought you said you'd safety-proofed the place—nothing listed in your name, no unit number, mail sent to a P.O. box, circuitous route to get there, cameras everywhere, multiple security systems."

"All that's true," she acknowledged. "But I'm still just sitting in a two-room box, stewing in my own anxiety. Why not let me be productive and work on the Penelope Wooten case? Then I'm not going crazy and I'm doing some good. Besides, like I said, I'm not sure Thurman even wants me dead. I think he may just want to reenter my life."

"Yeah, "Ryan interjected, "but it's not like he's some absentee father who just wants to take you to a ballgame. His version of 'reentering your life' might consist of abducting and torturing you."

"I didn't get that vibe from my conversation with Bolton Crutchfield," Jessie said.

"You didn't get that *vibe*?" Captain Decker repeated, borderline apoplectic. "You want me to release you back to work based on a vibe?"

"You weren't there, Captain," Jessie insisted, cautious not to share the true source of her confidence in her temporary safety. "Crutchfield made it pretty clear that he thought my father was looking for some kind of heartfelt reunion."

It was a fib, to be sure, but one she doubted the captain would follow up on. Ryan, however, was a different story.

"He's a serial killer, Jessie," he said, a perplexed look on his face. "He killed your adoptive parents. The idea that he just wants to reconnect in some genial, unthreatening way is … hard to accept."

"Look," Jessie conceded, "I'm not saying he wants to take me to Disneyland. I'm just saying that the combination of his intent being unclear and me climbing the walls if I can't do something constructive with my time justifies putting me back on the case."

Both men still looked unconvinced. But she sensed an opening and pressed.

"I would be surrounded by cops, Captain. Ryan would be there. So would Brady Bowen from West L.A. Station. Officer Beatty could tag along as my shadow. And we'd be in the Palisades, far from my usual jurisdiction. I'd probably be safer out there for the day than here. Come on; let me help solve this thing. There are two kids without a mother today. If I can help bring the person who did it to justice, you've got to let me try."

Decker scowled at her but she could see in his eyes that he was softening. After a moment, he spoke.

"Update her on the case, Hernandez," he muttered reluctantly.

"Sir," Ryan said," I just want to go on the record as saying I think this is a terrible idea."

"Noted. We're full up with terrible ideas today. Proceed with the update."

"Yes sir. First thing, we had to release Gray Longworth last night. He made bail and we couldn't keep him locked up unless we formally charged him with something substantial and we don't have enough to do that yet. But he's being watched to see where he goes now that he's out."

"Where are you thinking he might go?" Jessie asked.

"I'm not sure," he admitted. "But I can tell you one place he won't go—to dump the murder weapon. We found it yesterday."

Jessie couldn't hide her surprise.

"Where was it?"

"Funny you should ask. It was just off the running trail, not far from the edge of the Wooten property. An officer found it when he was asking other runners if they'd seen him the previous morning. No one had. Longworth claims he went the other way, up the Los Liones trail, rather than the more heavily trafficked East Topanga Fire Road, where the knife was found. We have no way of verifying or disproving that as of yet."

"Any luck with the knife?" Jessie asked. "Maybe a nice print or two?"

"Nope. It had been wiped clean. It was also doused in some bleach-like substance. So there wasn't even any blood residue on it. The only way we could verify it was the knife used was because the puncture wounds matched."

"Maybe the CSU folks can ID the brand of bleach," Jessie suggested. "That might help."

"They already did. It's a fairly obscure brand called Green Clean. It's supposed to be more eco-friendly. We thought that could narrow down our list of suspects. Even in a place like Pacific Palisades, it's hard to come by."

"Did the Wootens have it?" Jessie asked.

"No," Ryan said. "We looked everywhere."

"That's interesting," Jessie mused. "It suggests that even if this was a crime of passion, the cover-up wasn't. The killer had to take the weapon to another location to clean it, then dump it on the trail. Has anyone checked the Longworth house to see if they use it?" Jessie asked. "It was found on the trail, right? It follows that if Gray is our killer, he could have wiped it down and taken it on his run so he could dump it."

"It's definitely a possibility," Ryan agreed. "That's part of why we have someone on him; in case he tries to dump a bottle he hid somewhere. The house search turned up nothing."

"So where do we go from here?" Jessie asked.

"I was thinking we go back and talk to the wronged wife, Eliza Longworth."

"So now you're starting to share in my doubts about her?" Jessie asked, unable to keep the triumphant tone out of her voice.

"I didn't say that," Ryan argued. "I just figured we should talk to her when she isn't drugged up in a hospital. Maybe she won't seem so sympathetic when she's not in bed in a gown."

"I didn't find her all that sympathetic when she *was* in the gown," Jessie said.

"Wow, you really have it in for her, don't you?" Ryan marveled.

"I just think that a woman wronged by both her husband and her best friend might have an ax to grind. I know *I* was pretty pissed when I found out my husband was cheating. I'd cut her a little more slack if she just admitted to it and didn't play the martyr."

"Well," Ryan said, "maybe she'll own that a bit more when we talk to her today. I'm also hoping she can give us a little more insight into her husband. Somehow I don't think she'll be all that eager to protect his secrets after what he's done."

"There's that too," Jessie agreed.

"All right, you two," Captain Decker said, wrapping things up. "You can discuss strategy more on the way out there. God knows you'll have enough time. And you don't have to take Beatty with you. Hernandez, you and the detective from West L.A. should suffice. Now get out of here. I have other meetings."

He stood up and ushered them out of the office, his concerns about Jessie's well-being now taking a backseat to staying on schedule. They walked out into the bullpen as the door slammed behind them.

"Bathroom break and head out in five?" Ryan suggested brusquely.

"Sounds good," Jessie said. "I'll meet you in the main lobby."

As he walked off, she couldn't help but notice the chill between them, something she'd never felt before.

Chapter Twenty Six

For the first half of the trip to Pacific Palisades, they drove mostly in silence.

Jessie was happy for it, as she was navigating a complicated confluence of emotions. Part of her felt surprisingly light and cheery under the circumstances. She realized that was almost entirely due to the knowledge that her father wasn't an active threat to her safety, at least not for another ten hours.

With that in mind, she was able to keep her positive attitude. That is, as long as she didn't allow her thoughts to drift to the murder of her parents or to Xander's accusation: that she only became a profiler to rein in her own thirst for blood.

The truth was that this wasn't the first time that notion had entered her head. On more than one occasion she'd asked herself why she felt the need to work in a field where she interacted regularly with vicious, amoral murderers.

Her answer had always been that she had seen one up close, suffered at his hands, and didn't want others to go through the same thing. But somewhere, deep down, she'd always wondered if that was an excuse to loiter in this dark world.

There were, after all, other ways to help those who had survived brutal crimes. She could have become a victims' advocate or a mental health counselor or a criminal prosecutor. They all fought the good fight on behalf of victims. And yet she had chosen a career that required her to get into the minds of the most deviant killers around.

She had always believed it was because she had some special insight into how to stop them. But was it really because she felt a special kinship to them; because she understood them in a way most people didn't?

Jessie shook the thought from her head, deciding it was preferable to direct her thoughts elsewhere, even if that meant her attention drifted to the iciness that had developed between her and Ryan. She knew he was annoyed with her take on Eliza Longworth. But she sensed that wasn't the main reason he was troubled.

Even if Captain Decker hadn't picked up on it, he clearly knew that she wasn't being fully forthcoming about why she wanted to be working this case at all. Finally, unable to contain the roiling thoughts in her head, she spoke.

"Just spit it out," she demanded, louder than she'd intended.

"What?" he asked, startled by the sudden break in the stillness between them.

"You don't think I should be working the case."

"I thought I stated that pretty clearly back at the station," he pointed out.

"Yeah, but not for the same reason Decker didn't. You don't buy my explanation."

He looked over at her, sizing her up quickly before returning his eyes to the road.

"Are we being real here, Jessie?" he asked. "Are we at the point in our working relationship where we can be straight with each other without worrying about bruised feelings?"

"We are," she told him with certitude.

"Okay, then. You're right. I don't buy your story for one second. I believe you might be going stir-crazy in that apartment. That definitely tracks with what I know about you. But there is no way in hell you believe your father is only after a family reunion and means you no harm. There is a big, honking piece of information that you have—that you're not sharing—which makes you sure he's not coming after you. Otherwise, you'd be sitting on your couch with a gun pointed at your front door."

"I still don't have a gun," she noted petulantly, "thanks to the bureaucratic stylings of the Los Angeles Police Department."

"Don't deflect," Ryan countered. "You wanted to be real. This is me being real. You don't have to tell Decker. But don't you think I deserve to know what changed? Your parents were murdered less than two days ago. And yet, you look as untroubled as I've seen you since that day I lectured in your grad school class. Something has changed."

Jessie sat quietly for several seconds, turning over his words in her head. Finally, she came to a decision.

He's right. I owe him the truth. I just have to trust that he won't burn me.

"He left me a tape," she said softly.

"What?"

"Xander Thurman. I found a videocassette addressed to me in my parents' condo. I stashed it and brought it back here. I finally got to watch it last night."

Ryan looked like he had a million questions for her but finally settled on just one.

"What was on it?"

"I'll give you the short version because I'm still having issues processing the long version. Basically, he wants me to join him and become some kind family-style, super-serial-killing squad. He thinks the world needs a little unnatural selection and he's decided the Thurman brood should take up the task. I guess he thinks that I'm genetically predisposed to be like him. In fact, he basically said the only reason I became a profiler was so I could get up close to death and still be seen as normal."

"Okay," Ryan said slowly. "First—that is full-on psycho talk. Second—I don't see why you're more relaxed after having heard it."

"Because he gave me a deadline. I'm supposed to e-mail him to let him know if I'm in by tonight at eight p.m., which means that until then, I'm reasonably confident he won't try to murder me. So I've got that going for me, which is nice."

"Any chance of tracing the e-mail?" Ryan asked, notably not even addressing the idea that she might say yes.

"Unlikely. It's a generic Gmail account. He could look at my response from any library or internet café and be gone in two minutes. He could use an internet-enabled burner phone. He wouldn't have come up with this method without having thought it through."

"So we'll think of another way to catch him," Ryan said optimistically. "After all, we've got a full ten hours to figure this out."

Jessie felt an enormous, unexpected sense of relief at his words. She was glad to no longer carry the burden of this knowledge alone. And Ryan's seeming dismissal of even the notion that she might take Xander up on his offer reassured her in a way that made her feel guilty for ever doubting him.

"Yeah," she agreed. "We've got all the time in the world."

Twenty minutes later, they pulled up at Eliza Longworth's house. Brady Bowen was already waiting out front.

They were just about to get out when she got a text.

"Everything okay?" Ryan asked.

"Yeah. It's just a message from the funeral director in Las Cruces. Everything is set for Sunday. All I have to do is show up."

Ryan sat in the driver's seat, not saying anything. After a moment, he reached over and gave her hand a little squeeze. She looked over and saw that he was smiling at her.

They were interrupted by Brady rapping on Ryan's window.

"We doing this or what?" he asked.

Jessie couldn't help but chuckle at the guy's bull in a china shop style. Ryan nodded and opened the door as Jessie wiped away the tear that had appeared at the corner of her eye.

"What have we got here, buddy?" Ryan asked.

"Eliza Longworth is inside waiting."

"She have a lawyer with her?" Jessie asked.

"No," Brady said. "I wanted this to be more of a casual conversation. Did you have something else in mind, Jessie?"

"I wouldn't count on this being casual," Ryan muttered to him loud enough for her to hear.

Jessie didn't respond. Instead, she focused on taking in the Longworth house as they walked toward the front door. It was the first time she had seen the place. And while it wasn't as opulent as the Wooten home, it wasn't anything to sneeze at.

It was also built into the side of the hill and three stories tall, though the lower level looked smaller and squatter than the Wootens'. And while it wasn't a full-on mansion, it still had enough extravagance to make most folks jealous, including plantation-style pillars and a marble-slabbed porch. As they approached, she could see a pool in the backyard with a water feature that looked like a mini Niagara Falls.

Brady knocked on the door. While they waited for it to open, Ryan leaned over to quietly whisper to Jessie.

"Remember, we're here to get information, not throw bombs."

Jessie smiled back at him, but said nothing.

I'll get what I need, thank you very much.

CHAPTER TWENTY SEVEN

As soon as she opened the door, Eliza knew she was in for a rough time.

She vaguely remembered all three faces from their visit to the hospital the other day, though everything from that time, including their names, existed in something of a drug-induced haze.

But now, more aware and more apprehensive, she could see this was going to be a struggle. Both male detectives had fairly nonjudgmental expressions. But the woman's face was set hard, in something close to a grimace.

"Please come in," she said, trying not to feel intimidated.

"Thank you, Mrs. Longworth," the heavier, mustached man said. "You may not recall but I'm Detective Brady Bowen from LAPD's West L.A. Station. This is Ryan Hernandez from Central Station. He's a detective too. And this is Jessie Hunt, she's a profiler who consults for us. Do you remember talking to us at the hospital?"

"Kind of," Eliza said. "It's all a little cloudy."

"We understand," said the muscular, good-looking detective named Hernandez. "That's why we wanted to meet with you again, when you were more clear-headed. Do you mind if we ask you a few additional questions?"

"No. I'll do the best I can to help," she promised as she led them into her kitchen and motioned for them to take a seat at the breakfast table.

"Okay, great," Detective Hernandez said. "Can you walk us through your movements on the morning of the incident?"

Eliza tried not to react to him calling the death of her best friend "the incident." She knew he was just trying to be diplomatic. But it still felt wrong.

"Sure," she began. "I guess our morning was typical. Well, not *completely* typical. I had kicked my husband out of the house the night before for sleeping with my best friend. But as far as the daily routine goes, it was typical. The kids didn't know anything was different. I got them up—Millie is four and Henry is two— around six a.m., helped them get dressed, and made breakfast. We left around six forty-five for their preschool. It's about a ten-minute drive. I dropped them off and got back here soon after seven."

"What did you do after you got back?" the profiler named Jessie Hunt asked. Eliza noticed an edge in her voice that neither detective had.

"I prepped an art project for Millie's class," she said, pointing at a pile of papers on the family room table in the adjoining room. "I'm the volunteer art docent. We do a project every month and I was supposed to go in later that day. I was rushing to get the last-minute details ready."

"Then what?" Hunt asked, still curt.

"When I was done, I walked over to Penny's. I had texted her earlier that morning to let her know I was going to stop by before our yoga lesson, but she hadn't replied. I wanted to talk, just the two of us, so it wouldn't be so awkward with Beth around."

"Yes," Hunt noted sharply. "You mentioned at the hospital that you were going to tell her you didn't want to throw away years of friendship over her affair with your husband. That is amazingly gracious of you."

Eliza could see the other woman sizing her up and finding her lacking. She tried to remain calm, not wanting to show upset to a bunch of law enforcement officers. She felt like Hunt was baiting her, to see if she would lose it and somehow reveal that she was capable of unexpected bursts of rage. In addition to be being mean-spirited, Eliza thought it was also insulting.

"Look," she said, refusing to be worked, "I think I told you in the hospital, we were friends forever. I couldn't just throw all of that away. I mean, the night before I could have. But when I woke up the next morning I was less angry than sad. I felt like a huge chunk of who I was had been removed. And I wasn't ready to just toss it away forever. Can you understand that?"

"I'm trying to," Hunt said, less than convincingly.

Finally Eliza decided to push back.

"Look, Ms. Hunt. I get that you have to pursue every angle. But do you have to do it with such obvious disdain for me? I'm happy to answer all your questions. I'll provide you with whatever verification I can to confirm what I'm telling you. But maybe you could look at things from my perspective for half a second?"

"Mrs. Longworth..." Hunt started to say.

"No, wait," Eliza interrupted. "In the last few days, I found out that my oldest, dearest friend had been having an affair with the man I committed to spend my life with. Then, when I try to find a way to move past that and salvage the friendship, I discover that the girl I've loved like a sister since we were eight has been brutally murdered. I found her, Ms. Hunt. I fell in her blood. I tried to revive her. I held her body in my arms. And now you come in, all gangbusters, with your snide remarks and your turned-up nose. I get that you have to question me. I get that it's your job to be skeptical. But do you have to enjoy it so much?"

She stopped and took a deep breath, wondering if she had maybe gone too far. To her relief, Hunt looked at least mildly chastened.

"Look," Eliza continued more calmly now, "if you want, I'll take a lie detector test. I'll hand over my phone and e-mails, whatever will help. But can you understand how frustrating it is to try to defend myself against your insinuations while at the same time trying to keep my life from completely falling apart? My husband, who I kicked out of our home, spent a night in jail recently because he is being investigated for the same thing you're asking me about. Do you get how unsettling that is? My husband is a suspect in the murder of my best friend, who he was cheating with. That is not a sentence I thought I'd ever have to say, Ms. Hunt.

"Oh, and by the way, I still have two children to raise. They don't have a clue about any of this. They think Daddy is away on business. Millie, my older one, is best friends with Penny's daughter, Ana. She keeps asking me when they can have another play date. How am I supposed to answer that one? And meanwhile, life goes on. That art project I was supposed to teach on Tuesday was rescheduled for today. I'm supposed to go in and act like everything is normal for a bunch of four-year-olds. And that's happening in … oh god, I'm supposed to be there in less than an hour."

"Okay, Mrs. Longworth, just calm down," Detective Bowen said, not intending to sound condescending but failing. "We don't want to upset you and we don't you to be late for your daughter's art lesson. But we do have a few more questions, if you could accommodate us a bit longer."

Eliza went over to the cupboard, grabbed a glass, and poured herself some water. After chugging the whole thing, she felt composed enough to respond.

"Go ahead," she said.

"Thank you," he replied. "Is there anyone else who might have wanted to hurt Penny? Anyone unconnected to your … personal situation?"

Eliza had been in such a defensive crouch that she hadn't expected the question. A thought flashed through her head, one that hadn't occurred to her before. She was reticent to mention it but could tell from Jessie Hunt's expression that she'd picked up on the hesitation. So she shared something she thought she never would.

"Maybe," she said. "I didn't want to say this because it didn't seem relevant. And if I'm being honest, because, despite everything, I didn't want to sully her memory. But Penny had other affairs."

Both men looked at her with stunned faces. Hunt seemed less surprised.

"How would that sully her memory any more than it already had been?" Hunt asked, clearly making an effort to keep her tone neutral. "Hadn't it already been irreparably damaged by sleeping with your husband?"

"Yes, to me it had," Eliza admitted, "but from the outside, maybe not. When all the details of this come out, the public might view what she did to me as forgivable. Imagine the headline: *Woman falls for her best friend's husband, gives in to temptation in a moment of weakness.* But if she is revealed as a serial philanderer, then the world will just see her as a slut."

"Isn't there some truth to that?" Hunt asked carefully.

"Probably," Eliza conceded reluctantly. "But don't you see, that's not the point. Listen, I admit that after I learned about this, I hated them both. Maybe I shouldn't say that. I know it makes me look guilty. But it's true. I felt betrayed. I still do. It's like I'm writhing around in quicksand and even though it puts me at risk, I feel like lashing out.

"But when I get a few seconds to think clearly, I realize—that's not how I want Penny to be remembered, even after what she did to me. We had so many great years together. I want to hold on to those. I have to believe that more than two decades of friendship define who she really was, not the last month of her life. Besides, her kids don't need to live with that. They don't need their mommy branded with a scarlet letter. They're going to have a hard enough time trying to live without her, especially with Colton Wooten as their primary caregiver."

No one spoke for several seconds. Finally Detective Hernandez raised the question Eliza knew they'd get to eventually.

"Do you think Colton knew about her affairs?" he asked.

Eliza debated how forthright to be but then decided that at this point she might as well lay it all out on the table.

"Penny always said no. But I think that deep down he might have suspected it and just not wanted to know. He's an ambitious guy, political aspirations and all. If he knew the truth, he'd have to deal with it. If he only suspected, he could pretend not to know and treat everything as normal."

"And you think one of these affairs might have ended badly?" Hunt asked her.

"I don't know. We didn't really talk about it. I didn't want to give her the impression I approved of what she was doing, even if Colton is an asshole. But you asked if there might be other people to consider who might want to hurt her. I had to mention it, just in case."

"Is there any record of these affairs?" Detective Bowen asked. "How many she had? With whom?"

"I know she communicated with them through direct messages, using an anonymous Twitter handle. I'd see her on her phone sometimes. I don't remember the handle she used though."

"That's a problem," Detective Bowen said. "We can't get into her phone and her husband doesn't know her password."

"Oh, that's easy," Eliza said. "Her password is 265262. It's the numerical equivalent of "ColAna" for the kids, Colt Jr. and Anastasia."

"Thank you," Detective Bowen said. "We'll look into that."

"One more question for you, Mrs. Longworth," Detective Hernandez said, "and then we'll head out so you can get to your art lesson."

"Yes?" she asked, feeling her stomach tighten.

Isn't this when they ask the "gotcha" question that puts the wrongfully accused man on death row?

"Your husband says he was trail running at the time of the murder; that he parked near here. Did you see him?"

"No," Eliza answered, relieved that they finally seemed to have taken her at her word but conflicted about them apparently using her against her husband. "But that doesn't mean much. It would depend on where he parked and when. I could have easily missed him."

"He says he accidentally left his phone in the car and took the Los Liones trail route. Do you find those claims to be credible?"

Eliza thought about it.

"I could see him leaving his phone. He normally went on runs straight from the house. If he was leaving from the car, his routine might have been upset and he could have just forgotten it. Besides, reception is pretty awful in the canyons back there. He wouldn't have been able to use it for emergency calls. So unless he was planning to use his running app, he wouldn't have cause to take it."

"And what about his claim that he ran the Los Liones route?" Hernandez prodded, noticing that she hadn't answered that part of the question.

"Isn't there some rule against making a wife say something incriminating against her husband?" she asked. "Even if he is a bastard cheater?"

"Do you have something incriminating to say?" Hernandez asked, his eyebrows raised.

"I guess it's possible he took that route," she said.

"You sound skeptical," Hunt noted.

"It's just that he doesn't like the Los Liones trail because it's steep and he has bad knees. The East Topanga route is flatter so he prefers it. It doesn't mean he didn't take Los Liones. But knowing Gray, he wouldn't take it unless he could complain about it to me after. That's his big thing—complaining. I mean, this is a guy who complained when I asked him to do the laundry, saying he didn't know how. And considering that I'd just kicked him out of the house, he didn't have that incentive to run the more difficult route. So draw your own conclusions."

All three of her interrogators shared a look she couldn't interpret. She didn't know how much damage she'd done to Gray's alibi. But at the moment, she'd didn't really care. She had twenty four-year-olds waiting to do chalk drawings and she had no intention of keeping them waiting.

CHAPTER TWENTY-EIGHT

Jessie, Ryan, and Brady were in digital hell.

After Brady called Gray Longworth with a message letting him know they'd like him to come back in for additional questioning, they returned to the station, where the tech team had already accessed Penelope Wooten's phone. The three of them, seated at a large circular table, started going through her alternate Twitter feed. It was long, involved, and confusing.

"I'm happy to go out and bring Longworth in myself," Brady said after about thirty minutes of poring over the slang-heavy messages.

"No way," Ryan said. "You're not getting out of this task that easy. Besides, Longworth knows we want to talk to him. Let's let the anxiety build in him a bit before we go at him again."

Jessie looked up from her screen.

"Aren't you concerned that he might try to run?" she asked. "He has to know we can't verify his alibi. If he's the one who tossed the knife, he's probably worried we found it. And he was already on tenterhooks after his family life exploded. Do you really trust him to show up?"

"We still have an officer on him," Ryan assured her. "If he tries anything hinky, they can scoop him up. We'll get more out of him if he comes in voluntarily."

"I don't know," Brady said. "Jessie might be right. I really think I should go help that officer out."

"You are not getting out of looking through Penelope Wooten's messages," Ryan said emphatically. "I know modern technology scares your old-man sensibilities, but you're going to have to fight through it. Besides, this is *your* case. We're just helping you out."

"But these guys she's communicating with are so skeevy," Brady protested.

"Wow," Ryan countered. "If *you're* saying a dude is skeevy, then he must really be bad. After all, you're kind of skeeve personified."

"Don't be cruel," Jessie piped up. "Brady's not that skeevy. If he shaved his mustache, he'd look much less like a pedophile."

"Thanks for the support, Jessie," Brady said sarcastically.

One of the tech guys, tall and lanky, with pale skin and jet black hair that swooped down over his eyes, walked over and plopped down a sheaf of paper. He was wearing jeans and an old, black System of a Down concert T-shirt. Apparently he wasn't burdened by any kind of dress code.

"More work, Gregor?" Brady whined.

"Actually less," Gregor replied. "We used an algorithm to collate Penelope Wooten's direct messages. We eliminated anyone she communicated with fewer than three times. We figured anything less than that was just 'feeling out' stuff."

"That's pretty clever," Jessie noted.

"Thanks, we try," Gregor said drily. "But our unit actually likes to go above and beyond so we went a step further. Of the remaining messages, we pulled ones that included a specific date, time, or address. That dramatically reduced the relevant communications."

"By how much?"

"Down to this stack," Gregor said, pointing at the papers he'd dropped on the desk. "It looks like she had 'encounters' with approximately nine people since she joined Twitter in 2015. But of those nine, we've gleaned that six were only one-night stands."

"You are kind of terrifying me a little bit right now, Gregor," Brady said.

"You have nothing to fear if you have nothing to hide, Detective Bowen," Gregor shot back.

"So that leaves us with three longer-term affairs," Jessie said, getting them back on task.

"That's right," Gregor agreed. "I leave it to you highly trained professionals to draw conclusions about our remaining candidates. Here's their correspondence."

Gregor patted the stack and walked off, apparently neither needing nor expecting a thank-you.

"Shall we?" Ryan asked, grabbing the papers and doling them out evenly.

They each took two one-night stands and one long-term affair. Jessie began going through hers and pretty quickly dismissed both men that Penelope had only been with once. One of them had died of cancer in 2017 and the other moved to Indianapolis last year.

The one longer-term relationship on her list, a realtor from Sherman Oaks named Matt Stokely, also looked to be a bust. From what Jessie could glean, they had been involved from April to July of 2018 and met from six to eight occasions.

But based on his social media accounts, it appeared that Stokely had been at a Realtors convention in Santa Barbara from last Thursday through Sunday and had extended it into a vacation that was still going on. There were multiple time-stamped photos of him at a restaurant in town on Monday night and on Goleta Beach on Tuesday at around 11 a.m. The time window didn't completely eliminate him. But at least on initial inspection, Jessie doubted he was her man.

From his intermittent grunts, it sounded like Brady was having just as little luck. But after about fifteen minutes, Ryan looked up with a gleam in his eye that suggested pay dirt.

"I think we may have a live one. His name is Jeff Percival. And he does *not* seem like a quality dude."

"What do you mean?" Brady asked.

"First things first," Ryan said. "It looks like Penelope was seeing him from just after Thanksgiving until around the end of January of this year."

"That's still pretty fresh," Jessie noted.

"It would seem that Jeff agrees with you," Ryan said. "Because while there is no communication from Penny to him after January twenty-ninth, he continued to DM her repeatedly well into this month. And that's just on Twitter. This doesn't include e-mails or phone calls."

"Sounds like he handled her rejection in a gentlemanly manner," Jessie said.

"Yeah—not so much. Let's just say that Jeff does not like to be left hanging. That's borne out by the fact that he has one active restraining order against him from another woman. He was also convicted of a stalking violation with another woman four years ago."

"Where is Mr. Percival now?" Brady asked.

"He currently lives in a one-bedroom apartment off Wilshire in Santa Monica. Care to join me for a visit?"

"I'm up for it," Jessie said, leaping at the chance to get off desk duty.

"You know," Brady said, "I'm going to leave that to you two. I was kidding before. But I really am annoyed that Gray Longworth hasn't gotten back to me. I'm going to go to his office and let him know that his presence wasn't so much requested as demanded."

"Okay," Ryan said. "Things are looking up. We've got two scumbags to track down as potential murder suspects. That's more promising than when the day started."

As they left the station, Jessie leaned over and asked Ryan a question.

"Is it weird that we're both excited to visit the residence of a misogynistic stalker who might have killed someone? I feel like we're giddier than we should be."

"We can save that for therapy, Jessie. Right now I'm on a degenerate high. Don't bring me down."

CHAPTER TWENTY NINE

As they pulled up at the corner of Wilshire Boulevard and Stanford Street, Jessie reviewed Jeff Percival's file. It was pretty spotty since his last brush with the law, a restraining order filed last summer by a woman who worked at a restaurant Percival frequented. He had no current job listed and was in a dispute with his landlord about overdue rent payments.

"Ready?" Ryan asked.

"Yup. Let's go say hi."

"Okay. But since you're unarmed and you know, not a cop, I'm going to ask you to wait outside until I've verified he doesn't have a weapon."

"Details, details," Jessie teased as they approached Percival's complex.

She forced herself to take a few deep breaths and calm down. This was her first real field situation since the National Academy and she tried to remember not to get cocky just because she now knew a few moves.

Percival's place wasn't going to make either the Wootens or Longworths jealous. The two-story apartment complex was easily fifty years old, with exterior-facing doors and a crumbling cement stairwell leading to the second floor and his apartment. The units had bars on the windows and the smell from the nearby dumpsters made Jessie's eyes water. She wondered if Percival ever took Penelope back here.

Not exactly a babe magnet.

When they reached his door, Ryan had her wait several paces back as he knocked loudly, his hand resting on his gun holster.

"Jeff Percival," he called out. "LAPD. We need to speak to you. Open up."

There was no response from inside. He called out again.

"Percival, this is LAPD. Open the door now."

Still nothing.

A few seconds later, Jessie heard a high-pitched cry and swiveled around. After a moment, she relaxed. Half a block away, a woman was pushing a very unhappy baby in a stroller. She had just returned her attention back to Percival's door when she got an idea.

"Hey, Ryan," she whispered loudly. "You hear that crying?"

"Yeah," he said, not turning around. "What about it?"

"Are you sure it's not coming from inside the apartment? Can we be sure this guy didn't kidnap one of Penelope Wooten's kids?"

He glanced back at her and rolled his eyes. But as he did, he also smiled.

"Jeff Percival, we hear the crying in there," he shouted as he winked at her. "If you are holding a hostage, now would be the time to release them. Otherwise we're going to have to enter. You have five seconds."

As he said that line, he held up three fingers to indicate when they would really breach. Jessie nodded in understanding and prepared to follow him in.

"One," he began. "Two, three…"

Ryan kicked in the door just after "three" and rushed in. Despite his earlier instructions to wait outside, Jessie followed, feeling naked without any kind of weapon. She scanned the room as quickly and efficiently as possible. There wasn't much to see in the main room.

Percival had a loveseat against one wall with a beat up coffee table and television as the only other furniture. The small breakfast nook had a card table and two folding chairs. The kitchen, cramped and narrow, held no surprises.

By the time she'd finished surveying the room, Ryan was already entering the bedroom. She hurried after him and got to the doorway just as he was checking the bathroom.

"Closet was clear," he called out, apparently over the fact that she'd entered before he said it was safe. "Check under the bed."

Even though there was only about six inches of space between the bed and floor, Jessie knelt down and glanced underneath. There was lots of stuff there—food wrappers, dirty clothes, dust bunnies—but no people.

She got up and gave the bedroom a more fulsome examination. It was as pathetic as the living room, with an overflowing laundry hamper in one corner, a baseball bat beside the bed, and a massive, framed poster of Nickelback as the only art.

The poster rested along the wall next to the barred window and didn't even work as kitsch. The room was too dark to really see it and it hung about two feet lower than the standard sightline.

Why would he hang it that low?

She walked closer to the frame and noticed a surprising number of scrapes in the paint all over the wall near the edges of the frame, as if the thing had been hastily removed and replaced many times.

On instinct, she removed the frame from the wall. What she saw behind it made her gasp.

"What is it?" Ryan asked, rushing out of the bathroom.

She didn't need to reply for him to get it. He walked over and they both stared, trying to take it in.

On the wall was an array of photos of Penelope Wooten, some that she'd posed for, others that had clearly been taken surreptitiously. One showed her leaving the supermarket. Another was of her at the park with Colt and Anastasia. A third was of her in an evening gown at a black tie event with Colton. There were easily two dozen photos taped to the wall, each with borderline illegible penciled notes written next to them. One photo was of the Wooten house, with the address written below it.

"I really think we need to find Jeff Percival," Jessie said quietly.

"Already on it," Ryan said, pulling out his phone. "I'm going to call from outside. The reception is iffy in here."

As he walked out of the room, Jessie moved closer to the disturbing collage, trying to discern if there was any larger pattern to it. She could hear Ryan calling in the APB as she rose onto her tip-toes, trying to read one word written in large cursive letters under a photo that Percival had obviously taken while Penelope was sleeping. It took a second to get it, but she was ninety-five percent sure it said "Mine."

She was about to pull out her phone to take a photo of the wall when she noticed something odd. Even though he hadn't finished calling in the alert, Ryan had suddenly stopped talking. Then she heard it—what sounded like a pained, desperate grunt.

She shoved her phone back in her pocket and looked around the room. Her eyes fell on the baseball bat beside the bed. As quietly as she could, she hurried over, grabbed it, and moved to the bedroom door.

With the bat gripped tightly in her hands, she peeked around the corner. To her horror, but not her surprise, she saw Jeff Percival behind Ryan, his right arm locked tightly around the detective's neck as he punched him repeatedly in the kidney with his left fist.

Without thinking, Jessie stepped out into the room, swinging the bat behind her. Percival, whose back was to her, saw movement out of the corner of his eye and glanced over just in time to see Jessie swing the bat forward. Before he had time to react, it connected with the back of his left knee. There was a loud popping sound as he dropped to his knees, screaming loudly as he released his grip on Ryan's neck.

Jessie swung the bat back again, this time ready to clock Percival in the back of the head. But as she did, Ryan, who couldn't yet speak, held up his hand for her to stop. She froze the bat in midair as the detective kicked Percival onto his back and rolled him over. He swiftly cuffed the man, ignoring his howls.

"No need to overdo it," Ryan rasped. "You got him good enough the first time. He's gonna be limping for a year."

Jessie nodded and dropped the bat. Only then did she realize that her whole body was trembling. She tried to play it off as she hurried quickly past the two men, mumbling almost inaudibly.

"I need to get some air."

CHAPTER THIRTY

They drove back downtown as fast as they could without resorting to the siren.

Ryan and Jessie had been all set to follow the squad car taking Percival to the hospital when they got the call from Captain Decker. Facial recognition had a potential hit on her father. He wanted them to come back to look at the footage on the high-def monitor to see if Jessie thought it was him.

So Ryan had a CSU unit check out Percival's apartment and told the officers to take him to the hospital. Then he called Brady. He got voicemail so he passed along what happened, explained why they couldn't stick around, and suggested he meet Percival at the hospital to question him. It was already late afternoon so he promised they'd return in the morning to follow up.

They sat quietly for much of the drive back, both of them lost in their own thoughts. Finally, Ryan spoke.

"Thanks for taking that guy out. I was struggling there. He really caught me by surprise."

"No problem. I was happy to do it. And I do mean happy."

"I think you might have torn every ligament in his knee with that swing," Ryan marveled. "The Dodgers should give you a call."

"Nah, I'm too expensive," Jessie said, smiling for the first time since the incident. "Imagine what I could do if I ever got that gun."

"Still working on it," he replied.

"I'll believe it when it's in my hand," Jessie said, then realizing how cynical she sounded, quickly changed the subject. "You think he's our guy?"

"He looks good for it," Ryan said. "He could have easily seen Gray Longworth running on the trail that morning, planted the knife in an area where he knew we'd find it, and connect it to the cheating husband."

"Yeah," Jessie said. "It fits."

"Then why do you sound skeptical?" Ryan asked, looking over at her.

"It's just that it seems to fit too perfectly. I find messy more credible."

"Fair enough," he said. "Let's just see how it shakes out. How are you feeling, by the way?"

"I'm okay," Jessie said. "I was a little shaky right after but I'm good now."

"That's not what I meant. It's almost five p.m.—three hours until you're supposed to reply to your father. Is that carefree vibe you had earlier starting to fade at all?"

"Let's just say I wouldn't call myself as happy-go-lucky as I was a few hours ago," Jessie conceded.

"Have you decided how you're going to play it?"

"Yeah. I'm going to tell him to screw off."

"That's one way to go," Ryan said carefully. "Have you considered saying yes and asking for a meet? Maybe we could trap him."

Of course it was a good idea that made perfect investigative sense under normal circumstances. But these weren't normal circumstances. Jessie already felt like she was putting Ryan at risk by even telling him about the video.

But if she did exactly what Xander had prohibited and tried to set up some kind of elaborate sting operation, she feared it would backfire. Not only did she suspect he'd likely developed measures to uncover a move like that and counter it, trying something might put members of the squad at risk. He had threatened the lives of anyone who assisted her. If she let others help and they were killed, their deaths would be her fault.

"I actually have considered that," Jessie told him, deciding to go with a half-truth. "But I dismissed it pretty quickly. Xander's no fool. He'd know I was lying. He might hope that I'll eventually wear down and consider his psycho proposition. But he'd never buy the idea that, days after he killed my adoptive parents, I'd sign on to be bosom buddy serial killers. No—anything other than flat out rejection would seem suspicious."

"Okay, so what happens when you reject him?"

"I'm hoping he gets pissed and tried to convince me in person."

"That's your big plan?" Ryan demanded incredulously.

"Look, I don't have a big plan," Jessie replied, frustrated. "But I'm tired of playing the cat and mouse game with him. This is my way of taking it to him. He's far more likely to show himself if I snub him. And I'll never be in a better position to take him on than I am now. My place is secure. I have two cops staying there, covering my back. The department is using its resources to find him. Now is the time to get him."

"But if he's as smart as you say, won't he know all that?" Ryan pointed out. "Won't he wait until things have settled down to come to you?"

"I'm not sure he's capable of holding back, especially after the e-mail I intend to write him. It's going to be ... disrespectful."

"Can I make a suggestion?" Ryan asked, sounding almost nervous.

"Please."

"Tell Decker about the videotape. If he knows the threat to you is imminent, he can provide additional resources. Let him help."

"Ryan, I can't tell him about the tape," she said. "What I did could be construed as stealing evidence."

"Not necessarily. You don't have to be *completely* forthcoming. Just shade the truth a bit. Tell him you saw a video in the VCR, figured it was old family movies, and took it to reminisce. It wasn't until later, when you were taking it out again to play it, that you noticed the Post-it and realized who it was from. That's completely plausible."

"Maybe."

"Jessie," Ryan said delicately. "I think we both know there's another reason you're hesitant to show Decker the tape, why you haven't even offered to let *me* see it."

"What reason is that?" Jessie asked, sounding more defensive than she intended.

"Come on, Jessie," he said, quietly coaxing her.

"Fine," she relented. "Maybe I don't want my boss and the people I work with to hear what Xander Thurman said. Maybe I don't want everyone around me to think I only became a profiler so I could be around the violence and death."

"Do you really think that your co-workers would believe that?" Ryan asked.

"Could you blame them?" she demanded. "It's in my blood, right?"

"If that's how it worked, every criminal's child would be a criminal too."

"We're not talking about a bank robber here," Jessie reminded him. "We're talking about a guy who gets off on torturing and murdering other human beings."

"Jessie," Ryan said quietly but with conviction. "You are not defined by who your father is. Don't let him try to convince you otherwise. He's just trying to get in your head. No one who works with you believes that you're like him. The real question is, do you?"

Before she could reply, Ryan's phone buzzed. He put it on speaker.

"Hey guys," Brady said. "How's everything going? It sounded like you had to bail in a hurry."

"The captain needed us on another pressing case," Ryan told him, steering clear of specifics. "Sorry to leave you holding the bag."

"That's okay," Brady replied. "Unfortunately, I've mostly got bad news to share."

"Lay it on us," Ryan said. "We're all about bad news today."

"Okay, well, first, I spoke to Jeff Percival, who will be in a leg cast for six weeks, by the way. He didn't deny an obsession with Penelope Wooten. But he claims he was in Mexico since last Saturday. He was uncomfortably chatty. He even told me that he hired multiple prostitutes who looked like Penelope while he was down there. But he said he only returned today—that he had just gotten back to L.A. when he found an intruder in his apartment."

"Oh great. So this guy is going to try to sue us now?" Ryan said.

"I wouldn't worry about it," Brady assured him. "He *did* have a collection of photos of a recently murdered woman hidden on his wall. I think you'll get the benefit of the doubt on this one."

"Does his story hold up?" Jessie asked.

"So far, yes. There was a duffel bag with dirty clothes in his car, along with several receipts on the floor. They're from Tijuana and some are time-stamped from earlier this week. We're also checking with Customs and Border Protection. In addition to checking driver's licenses, they track all license plates of vehicles that pass through the San Ysidro crossing near San Diego. It'll take a few hours but they should be able to verify if he crossed and when. We'll hold him based on the assault charge against Ryan but it looks like he may alibi out on the killing. And to be honest, when I mentioned Penelope Wooten's death, he seemed genuinely shocked by the news."

"Damn," Ryan said. "I thought we had the guy."

"If it's any consolation," Brady offered, "it sounds like Percival was well on his way to doing what someone else did first,"

"It's no consolation," Jessie said. "There's still a killer out there."

"Speaking of that, here's the other bad news. We lost Gray Longworth."

"What?" Jessie and Ryan said in unison.

"When I went to his office in Venice, they told me he cut out early for the afternoon. But somehow the officer watching him missed it. Maybe he wasn't paying close attention because he didn't expect him to leave so early. Whatever the reason, when I stopped by, Longworth was gone and the officer didn't have a clue."

"What about tracking his phone?" Jessie asked.

"I tried that first thing. It's off—has been for hours. It could have just died or he could have done it intentionally to evade us. We're checking his last known GPS coordinates and trying to get a court order to check his communications today. Maybe he sent an e-mail or text that hinted at where he was going. Either way, he's been in the wind for hours. We have units out looking for his car and tech is checking for pops on his credit or ATM card. Otherwise we're in wait-and-see mode."

"Maybe we should give the border patrol *his* info," Ryan suggested, only half-joking. "We could have one suspect leaving Mexico while another tries to make a getaway there."

"It's not a crazy idea, actually," Brady noted. "When I get off with you, I think I'll reach out to them."

"We're actually almost back to Central Station now," Ryan told him. "So we'll let you go. But keep us apprised, all right?"

"You got it. Have a good night," Brady said and hung up.

They made the final turn before entering the station's parking garage. Ryan looked over at Jessie.

"Time's almost up," he said. "Have you decided? Are you going to let Decker know what's going on?"

Jessie sighed and nodded.

"What do I have to lose? It's only my career, right?"

CHAPTER THIRTY ONE

D ecker wasn't as upset as she'd expected.

It wasn't clear whether he totally bought her "I inadvertently took what turned out to be crucial evidence" excuse. But he didn't call her on it. Once he was assured that Thurman's face wasn't visible in the video, his interest waned.

"You can bring it in tomorrow and we'll have tech see if they can glean anything you might have missed. You'd be amazed what they can pull from a seemingly useless piece of footage. In the meantime, I want you to take a look at the screen grabs of the guy we identified and see if you think it's your father."

A tech named Nora pulled up the footage. It was of a man exiting the 7th Street Metro Center station this morning at 10:19. He wore a cap and sunglasses and kept his head down most of the time he was on camera. But at one point, someone passing by accidentally bumped into him, causing him to look up briefly.

It was that moment that had been flagged by the facial recognition program. The clearest frame grab of his face had been isolated and cleaned up and was now staring back at her through the computer monitor. According to the readout on the screen, it matched older photos of Thurman with 82% accuracy. She stared at the man for a long time before answering.

"I just don't know, Captain," she admitted. "It could be him. Clearly the program thinks it might be. And it makes sense. How far is that metro station from where we are now—about a mile? But I haven't seen the man in anything other than grainy footage in which he's wearing disguises or masks for two years. The cheekbones look similar. But I can't honestly say how much of this is objectively judging and how much is me making assumptions."

Decker looked frustrated but said nothing.

"Were you able to track where he went after that?" Ryan asked Nora.

"No," she said. "We didn't get the image alert until about two hours ago so we couldn't track him in real time. We've had folks combing through camera footage from the area ever since. But our coverage has gaps in that sector. I wouldn't count on getting much back."

"So where do we go from here?" Jessie asked.

"Where *you're* going is home," Decker said firmly. "Nettles and Beatty will accompany you again tonight. Once you send out your e-mail reply to Thurman from the security of your apartment, we'll have our friendly tech folks here see if they can track down his location when he opens it. We'll probably increase patrols in your neighborhood overnight as an extra precaution. We may even add a couple more plainclothes officers at your building starting tomorrow. I just need to get authorization on that but I doubt it will be hard. In the meantime, we'll continue to scrub camera footage to see if he pops up again."

Jessie opened her mouth, ready to object, when Ryan, who was watching her closely, jumped in.

"I think that's a good plan, Captain," he said, staring her down as he spoke. "I'm sure Jessie will be a bit frustrated being in lockdown at her place. But she knows it's the right move at this point. I can knock out the paperwork on our arrest of Jeff Percival so she can head out now."

"Then we're agreed?" Decker said, looking at Jessie to see if she was on board.

She swallowed hard, telling herself that everything they were suggesting was reasonable. Just because it made her a passive participant in her own life didn't mean it wasn't the wisest course of action. She would still set everything in motion with her e-mail. She just wouldn't control what happened after that.

"Yes sir," she finally said, forcing a smile to her lips.

"Great," Decker said. "I'll notify Nettles and Beatty to close up shop here. You can head home in the next ten minutes. And remember to call in before you're about to hit 'send' on that e-mail. When do you plan to do it?"

"I was thinking seven fifty-nine, just to screw with him."

"Always smart to antagonize a serial killer," Decker replied drily before dismissing them all. Once the meeting broke up, Ryan motioned for Jessie to meet him in the courtyard.

"I'm sorry I bulldozed you back there," he said when they were outside. "But Decker's mind was made up. And I worried that if you balked at his plan, he'd start to wonder why. You don't want that, especially after you just told him what Thurman wants you to do."

"I thought you said no one would believe that I would ever consider accepting my father's proposition."

"I don't," Ryan assured her. "But he might think that you're emotionally compromised, which isn't a crazy concern. And you demanding to do something foolish, like act as bait, might make him question your judgment."

"I wasn't going to suggest that I serve as bait," Jessie protested.

"It never crossed your mind?" Ryan said, his eyebrows raised.

"Barely at all," she said, trying to fight off the smile she felt creeping to the edges of her mouth.

"Well, then, that's my bad, I guess," he replied, breaking out into a full-on grin.

"Yes, it is," she scolded playfully.

"Listen," he said, getting serious again. "I wanted to let you know my plan for the night. After I do this paperwork, I'm going to the gym for a bit. I need a good sparring session to build up my confidence after Percival got the jump on me today. Once I shower and clean up, I thought I might stop by a little later to see how you're holding up, maybe give one of the other guys a short break. Would that be all right?"

"Yeah," she said. "I'm happy to have the extra company. Nettles and Beatty are great, but neither is a sparkling conversationalist.

Just don't forget that shower. I don't need you stinking up my brand new cell, er, I mean, home."

He looked like he was going to respond, then seemed to change his mind as his face turned slightly pink. Jessie wondered what he was thinking at that moment but decided not to ask.

"I'll see you later then," he said and walked off, before turning back and adding, "Be safe."

Jessie watched him go, confused by what had just happened.

I wish they'd taught me how to profile that at the FBI.

Chapter Thirty Two

Both Nettles and Beatty seemed more comfortable wending their way through the labyrinthine route from the retail center to her apartment building this time around. Beatty only missed the boiler room door once this time, for which Jessie gave him a mocking slow clap. He flipped her off in response. They got to the building lobby just before 7 p.m.

"I'll take the first shift down here," Nettles said. "I'll check in with security to see if they have any updates. Beatty, you escort Jessie upstairs. Give me the all-clear when you're safely inside with the doors locked and security reengaged."

"Sounds good," Beatty said. "When do you plan to come up?"

"I probably won't hang out down here more than a couple of hours. I want to be in lockdown mode by nine p.m. unless there's an objection. Maybe I can even FaceTime my kids before bed."

"No objection from me," Jessie said. "Detective Hernandez said he might stop by later on to check in. But other than that, I'm happy calling it an early night. Today was a bear."

"Okay then," Nettles said. "See you in a bit."

He headed down the small set of stairs to meet Fred the security guard and Jimmy the doorman. They saw him coming, both looking visibly happy to have someone new to interact with. Jessie and Beatty went down the back hall to take the service elevator.

As it rose from the first floor to the fourth, Beatty removed his gun and held it in the ready position. Jessie stared at him. He saw her expression and smiled.

"Just precautionary," he said reassuringly.

"Hey, I'm not complaining," Jessie said.

The doors opened and Beatty stepped out first. They both scanned the long hallway for anything suspicious but it was empty.

"Let's go," Beatty said quietly. "No point in dawdling."

They hurried down the hall. When they got to Jessie's door, she checked the peephole to see if anyone had tried to enter. It was green. She unlocked the door and stepped inside with Beatty right behind her.

As she locked the door and went through the process of deactivating and reactivating security codes, he moved quickly through the apartment, turning on lights, checking behind doors, the closets, the bathroom.

"All clear," he said just as Jessie turned the perimeter alarm back on.

"Good to know," she said, peering through the peephole one more time.

"Nettles," Beatty said into the radio behind here. "Beatty here, over."

"Go ahead, Beatty."

"We're good up here. Unit is clean and we're back in lockdown mode."

"Excellent," came Nettles's voice. "All clear down here so far. Security reports nothing unusual. I'm going through footage of today's deliveries to see if anyone looks familiar. Otherwise it's quiet."

"Okay. We're going to settle in up here. I'll let you know when Jessie sends that e-mail."

"Roger that," Nettles said.

"So," Beatty said, turning to Jessie. "You got any more of that pizza?"

Jessie changed her mind at 7:28.

She knew it altered the original plan, but the idea of waiting another half hour to send an e-mail telling her father to screw himself was making her increasingly anxious. Better to just get it over with. She told Beatty as much and went into the bedroom to write a draft.

She sat down at her laptop and worked through several iterations before finally coming up with something she was happy with. The version she ended up with was short and to the point. It read:

Let me be clear. You are a killer who murdered the only real family I've ever known. We are nothing alike and I would never join your sick mission. Do the right thing. Turn yourself in.

She reread it a few times. It wasn't literature but it got the point across. She called the tech folks at the station to let them know she was about to hit "send." She did the same with Ryan but got his voicemail. He must have still been sparring.

"I'm about to send this," she called out to Beatty in the other room. "You want to give Nettles a heads-up?"

"Will do," he called back, coming to the door as he radioed down. "Nettles, Beatty here; over."

"Go ahead, Beatty."

"Jessie's tired of waiting around. She's sending the e-mail now."

"Understood."

"We'll let you know if we get a reply," Beatty said.

"Got it. Good luck, Jessie."

Jessie smiled.

"She says 'thanks,'" Beatty said.

Jessie reviewed the message one last time. Satisfied, she hit "send."

"It's done," she said, looking up.

"Want a celebratory slice of pizza?" Beatty asked. "It's almost ready to come out of the oven."

"I'm not super hungry," she replied. "Part of me wouldn't mind a celebratory shot of whiskey, but that seems like a bad idea."

"Maybe once we catch him," Beatty suggested. "In the meantime, don't let me eat alone. At least hang out with me."

Jessie got up, bringing the laptop with her to the breakfast table. She sat down as he took the pie out of the oven and started cutting it up. Then he got a plate for his three slices.

Though she knew there was no point, Jessie kept refreshing her e-mail. Of course there was nothing. It had been two minutes, hardly enough time to even open and read a message, much less reply.

"I feel bad," Beatty said as he took a big bite of pizza, trying to suck up a loose strand of ropy cheese. "Poor Nettles is looking at surveillance footage while I'm chowing down. I thought the junior officer always got the raw deal."

"Well, invite him up," Jessie suggested. "If he's done looking at the footage, there's no reason he has to stay down there until nine. That time seems arbitrary."

"Okay, I'll suggest it. But he's kind of a stickler so don't hold your breath."

Jessie nodded, eyeing the pizza even as she told herself she didn't need any.

"Nettles," Beatty said into the radio with a full mouth, "Beatty here; over."

There was no response. After waiting a few seconds, Beatty swallowed and tried again.

"Nettles, Beatty here; over."

The only sound on the other end of the radio was static mixed with intermittent crackling.

"Nettles, this is Beatty. Please respond. Over."

Still, there was nothing.

Beatty looked up at Jessie. His eyes suggested that he didn't think this was just a radio issue.

"Try again," she said urgently.

"Nettles, this is Beatty. I need you to respond now. Confirm your status, please. Over."

They waited a good ten seconds. Nothing.

Beatty, who had been staring at the radio as if willing it to respond, looked up at Jessie.

"I'm going down," he said.

CHAPTER THIRTY THREE

Jessie didn't try to talk him out of it. Despite her misgivings, she knew it was useless.

"I'll call it in," she said.

"It's probably nothing," Beatty said unconvincingly. "I bet he just went to the bathroom and forgot the radio."

"That doesn't sound like Nettles."

"No, it doesn't," he agreed.

"Be careful," she said. "If this is Thurman, he's adept with disguises. Don't trust anyone you come across, no matter how innocuous they look, okay?"

"Believe me, I'm not taking any chances. You want to check those cameras for me before I step into the hall? I'd rather not go out there blind."

Jessie turned the TV to the channel that had her security feed. According to the various cameras outside, the hallway was clear.

"You're good," she told him.

"Okay. Lock up again the second I step outside. And call it in ASAP. Better to deal with a false alarm than ... something else."

He unlocked the door and stepped into the hall as Jessie relocked the doors and punched the code back in. She grabbed her cell phone and dialed the station as she watched Beatty walk down the hall, gun out. He skipped the elevator and went to the stairwell, pushing the door open slowly. As he disappeared behind it, someone came on the line.

"Central Station," came a brusque female voice.

"Yes, this is criminal profiler Jessie Hunt. Please give me Captain Decker. This is an emergency."

"Connecting," the voice said without hesitation. She must have been alerted about the evening's situation because there was no pushback.

The call went to straight to Decker's office voicemail. Apparently the desk officer hadn't been informed of the nature of the situation after all. Jessie left a quick message explaining her concerns, hoping the call would be forwarded to his cell, as many cops set up their systems to do.

She tried calling the tech line and got voicemail for them too. Rather than leaving another message, she hung up and decided to just cut to the chase and call 911. She was immediately put into a hold queue. As she waited, she put the call on speaker, slid on her sneakers, and grabbed the nightstick beside the door.

Suddenly the call went dead. She walked over and looked at the phone screen. There were no signal bars. She glanced over at her laptop and saw that the screen now said "internet connection lost." She looked over at the TV.

The hallway images, in four boxes showing different angles, were still up. But as a precaution, that connection was hardwired and independent of the web for this very reason. She switched channels and got a blank screen. The only channel that worked was the one that wasn't internet-connected.

She was just starting to question whether this could be a coincidence when she saw movement at the end of the hall on the screen. Looking closely, she saw someone stumble out of the elevator. It was Nettles.

He was staggering down the hall with both hands clutching his throat. Blood was visibly seeping through his fingers. Jessie started for the door, then forced herself to hold back. She turned her attention back to the screen, looking for any additional movement in the elevator. Was Thurman hiding in there, hoping she'd open the door so he could attack?

Though it pained her, she waited until Nettles was almost to her door before unlocking it, her eyes on the monitor the whole time. He was just raising his hand to knock when she opened it and pulled him in. She gave one quick glance down both ends of the hall before closing and locking the door and turning the alarm back on.

Nettles seemed to be trying to speak but his efforts were in vain.

"Don't try to talk," she said as she laid him down on the floor and rushed to the kitchen to grab a roll of paper towels.

She pulled his hands away from his throat so she could get a better look. It took several seconds to dab away enough of the blood to see what was going on. His throat had been slit by a large, sharp knife. The incision was wide but not especially deep. She was no expert but it didn't appear that the carotid artery had been cut.

"Was it Thurman?" she asked.

Nettles nodded weakly.

As she pressed on his throat with a wad of paper towels, Jessie felt the gears clicking in her mind. Whatever else he was, Xander Thurman was not an amateur. If he had wanted to kill Nettles, he would have. So why did he let him live?

Nettles coughed and a spray of red mist shot out from the opening in his neck. The wound was now bleeding more profusely.

"Hold on," she said to Nettles. "I'm going to get something to tie this off."

She ran to the coat closet and pulled out a scarf. On her way back, she saw the land line phone and picked it up to call 911. There was no dial tone. Had Thurman cut the phone lines too?

As she wrapped her scarf tightly around Nettles's neck, she noticed that his weapon was missing. Movement out of the corner of her eye made her glance at the TV monitor again. The stairwell door at the end of the hall was slowly opening. And that's when she realized why her father had let Nettles live.

He didn't know which unit she lived in. Somehow he'd found her building but he couldn't be sure which apartment was hers. So he had let Nettles "get away" so he could watch where he went on the security monitor in the lobby. And now that he had found it, he was coming for her.

CHAPTER THIRTY FOUR

A cold chill went down Jessie's spine.

She watched the TV monitor, frozen in fear, as a figure stepped through the stairwell door into the hallway. He walked slowly and methodically down the corridor. A ski mask covered his face except for his mouth and eyes, but she knew it was him. She recognized the tall, lean frame.

She suddenly flashed back to a formless memory from her childhood, of her father walking toward her as she sat strapped to that wooden chair in the cabin. This man walked the same way, leaning slightly forward as he moved, as if propelled by some exterior force stronger than himself, guiding him down his brutal path.

Another cough from Nettles pulled her out of her nightmare reverie. She looked down at him. He couldn't speak but his eyes seemed to be saying "get out." He wanted her to leave him and escape. But there was nowhere to go. Xander was almost to the door. She couldn't jump out the window from forty feet up. Even if she survived, she'd simply be lying on the sidewalk with broken legs waiting for him to come down and finish her off. She was trapped.

That's not true.

She remembered now what she'd been too terrified to recall moments earlier. There was another way out—the shaft with the rope ladder hidden by her bathroom closet. It was intended for just this kind of scenario.

She looked down at Nettles again, whose eyes were fluttering. He seemed to be barely conscious. There was no way she could get him down that narrow shaft. Even if she was strong enough, he'd never survive all that jostling and banging.

She looked at the monitor again. Her father was right outside the door. He was staring at it, unmoving. She knew that it would require more than just a swift kick to get it open. She had time, if she would just get her ass in gear.

Jessie stood back up and looked down at Nettles, whose eyes were open again, though they looked hazy.

"I'm going to have to leave you here," she said quietly. "But I promise I'll come back."

She didn't wait for his acknowledgment as she grabbed him by the arms and dragged him into her bedroom. She pulled him around to the far side of the bed, where he wouldn't be visible from the bedroom door, then returned to the living room.

Xander was no longer staring at the door. Instead, he seemed to be pressing something against it. Jessie moved closer to the monitor and saw that it was some kind of putty. When he pulled several wires out of his pocket, she realized what he was doing: setting an explosive. He wasn't going to try to knock the door down. He was going to blow it up.

Jessie knew she didn't have much time. She grabbed the nightstick off the breakfast table, shoved her still-useless phone into her pocket, and was about to return to the bedroom when she had an idea.

Maybe she couldn't call for help. But there was another way to get it to arrive. As quickly as she could, she moved one of her chairs into the center of the living room. Then she rolled up a thick wad of paper towels, turned on a stove burner, and lit the wad. The end immediately burst into flames.

She hurried over to the chair, stepped onto it and held the burning end up to the sprinkler. It took about seven seconds for the sprinkler to turn on and begin to scatter water throughout the room. At the same time, the fire alarm went off, sending a loud wailing echo throughout the building.

She looked over at the TV screen and saw that her father was smiling. She didn't know if he was proud or amused. Either way, even as water sprayed down on him, he quickly resumed work on the explosive. He looked to be almost done.

She turned off the TV, grabbed the nightstick, and ran to the bedroom, where she closed the door, locked it with a deadbolt and chain, and then dropped the security bar down. After that, she moved to the bathroom and repeated the routine, fleetingly wondering how many people had chains, deadbolts, and security bars on their bathroom doors.

She opened the closet door, undid the hidden clasp on the left side, flipped the latch, and tugged on the shelving unit, which swung open to reveal the shaft and rope ladder attached to the brick wall behind it.

She shoved the nightstick into the back of her pants, stepped out onto the ladder, and pulled the shelving unit closed until she heard it click. Now completely surrounded by darkness, she made her way down the flimsy ladder as quickly as she safely could. With each cautious step, the sound of the fire alarm became more distant. She could see the dim laundry room light below and was almost to the bottom when she heard the explosion. Thurman was almost certainly in her apartment now.

She dropped the last few feet to the ground and scurried through the tiny crawl space out into the laundry room. A thirty-something guy who was pouring liquid detergent into a washer yelped when he saw her appear out of nowhere. The fire alarm wasn't audible down here and there was no water coming from the ceiling. Apparently folks doing their laundry were on their own in a fire.

"There's an intruder in the building," she said as she moved briskly past him. "Go next door to the coffee shop and call nine-one-one."

He stared at her dumbly.

"Do it!" she yelled before running out the door and up the stairs to the lobby level. When she emerged, she saw that the floor was soaked with water from the sprinklers. Residents were emerging from the elevators and stairwell and filing out of the building, confused by the combination of water, noise, and broken glass, likely caused by the explosion they'd just heard.

Jessie ran to the security station, pushing past bewildered tenants. When she got to the desk, she saw Fred the security guard lying on the floor in a pool of blood coming from his neck. Apparently, Xander hadn't been as delicate in how he handled him.

On the ground next to him was Jimmy the doorman. He wasn't bleeding as badly but the small bit that was coming from the back of his head told her that he had fared no better. It appeared that Xander had jammed the knife into the back of his skull.

She looked away quickly, trying to push the horror around her out of her mind. She would mourn these men later. Right now she had a job to do. On the ground beside Jimmy's body was a gun. She recognized it as the standard-issue weapon for LAPD uniformed officers. It must have been Nettles's. She picked it up.

A scream from somewhere in the crowd made her look up. Two women were leaning over a man lying on his back, unmoving.

Beatty!

She ran over and pushed her way through the rubbernecking crowd to get to him. He was bleeding from the back of the head, just like Jimmy. She felt a howl of grief begin to rise in her chest when he suddenly groaned.

"Beatty, you're alive!" she said, clasping his hands in hers. She looked at his head. It seemed that the blood was the result of blunt force trauma and not a stabbing.

"Jessie," he mumbled borderline intelligibly.

"I'm here," she told him.

"Thurman's here," he muttered.

"I know. He's in my apartment. I'm going back up. Are you okay?"

"Wait..." he whispered. "Wait for backup."

"I can't," Jessie said. "Nettles is up there, He's hurt bad. Xander will kill him when he finds him. I've got to go."

Beatty tried to grab her wrist as she stood up but she shook free. She turned to one of the women who had screamed earlier.

"He's a cop," she said. "Get him outside. Take care of him. Call nine-one-one. When help arrives, tell them to go to the fourth floor. And warn them to be careful. There's a killer up there."

The woman opened her mouth to speak but

Jessie was gone before she got a word out.

CHAPTER THIRTY FIVE

Jessie was short of breath.

The elevators weren't working so she had to take the stairs. The combination of sprinting up them and her heart beating almost out of her chest had her gasping for air.

She pushed open the fourth-floor stairwell door and peeked out. It was seemingly devoid of people but a thick cloud of smoke made visibility difficult. She crouched down low, trying to remember her training from the academy.

Most of it was hazy, but she knew she was supposed to look for potential hiding spots from threats, stay aware of what was behind her, and not fire her weapon until she was certain her target was a source of danger.

She moved carefully, her eyes darting everywhere as her back hugged the same wall as her door. A shadow emerged from the smoke and she raised Nettles's gun, flicking off the safety. Her finger lingered on the trigger as she tried to determine what was coming at her.

She was just about to fire when an older woman, a neighbor she saw occasionally but had never spoken to except to say hello, emerged from the smoke. She was clutching a small dog in her arms and looked bewildered. Jessie lowered her gun and waved the woman over.

"Go down the stairs at the end of the hall and exit the building," she whispered. "The elevators are inoperable. Do you understand?"

The woman nodded and did as she was told, disappearing once again into the thick smoke. Jessie was just returning her attention back in the direction of her apartment when she was knocked to the ground by a second explosion.

Her ears were ringing. As she pulled herself back up to a sitting position, she tried to get her bearings. After a few moments, she started to stand up, using one hand to steady herself against the wall while the other gripped the gun tightly.

Why was there another explosion?

She pictured Xander in her apartment and wondered what would cause him to use a second explosive. It only took a second for her to understand. He hadn't been able to access her bedroom and had used the same technique he'd employed on the front door.

The realization gave her a sudden surge of hope, the first she'd felt since she'd initially seen Nettles clutching his bloody throat. If he'd just set off the explosion at her bedroom door, then she had a significant, if brief, advantage. Xander thought she was in her bedroom and she knew that's where *he* was. He didn't have a clue as to her location but she knew his exactly.

She rushed to her door, moving as fast as she could while being half-blinded by the gray noxious cloud all around her. When she reached what was left of it, essentially a big gaping hole that extended about fifteen feet across, she stopped, allowed herself the briefest second to regroup, and then swung her body right so that she was facing into the remnants of her apartment, her gun raised, her eyes hunting for any movement.

It was too smoky to see much but she ducked down anyway, scurrying along the charred breakfast bar until she was able to peek around it in the direction of her bedroom. That's when she saw him.

Xander Thurman stepped through the husk of her bedroom into the living room. He was no longer wearing the ski mask and she could see him clearly. He held a long hunting knife in his right hand. His once black hair was littered with spots of gray. His face, still surprisingly youthful, was only just starting to develop the wrinkled lines appropriate to his age. His bright green eyes shined with the same, frenzied energy she remembered from when she was little, when he was consumed by enthusiasm for what he was doing. He looked ... happy.

Jessie stood up and pointed her gun at him. He saw her and turned to face her directly. She couldn't help notice that the man she'd once considered a giant was now only a few inches taller than she was.

"Drop the knife, interlace your fingers behind your head, and get on your knees," she ordered, her voice clear and firm.

He smiled at her, seemingly unsurprised to see her.

"Junebug," he said affectionately, apparently untroubled by the sight of his daughter pointing a gun at him. "It's been too long. You have no idea how long I've been searching for you. And now, finally, reunion!"

"I'm glad you're in such high spirits," Jessie said. "I'm more than happy to reminisce once you're cuffed and behind bars. All you have to do is drop the knife, interlace your fingers behind your head, and get on your knees. Do it now!"

"Is this any way to treat your long-lost daddy?" Thurman asked, taking a step toward her. "How can we be a big, happy family again if you treat a loved one in this manner?"

"I am going to end this reunion fast with a bullet in your forehead if you don't do as I say. I won't ask again—knife, fingers, knees. Now!"

"Okay, okay," he replied, dropping the knife so that it landed upright with the tip jutting out of the floor. "I suppose I shouldn't be surprised that you want brains splattered all over the place. It's that familial bloodlust rearing its head, I guess. See, Junebug, we're not so different."

"I'm nothing like you," she told him.

The smile faded from his lips and the next time he spoke, his voice was hard.

"You are exactly like me," he said, his voice ice cold.

There was a loud beep from the bedroom that made both of them turn their heads. Then Xander returned his attention to Jessie again and smiled.

"Oh, right," he said. "I guess you're not in the bathroom after all. You better duck."

Jessie had half a second to process that Xander had set another explosive on her bathroom door before everything around her burst into a tornado of fire and debris.

When Jessie got her bearings again, Xander Thurman was nowhere to be found. If she was lucky, he'd been blown to bits.

She grabbed hold of what was left of the breakfast bar and pulled herself to her feet. The gun was missing and flames licked the ceiling and walls of the apartment.

She wanted to go into the bedroom and grab Nettles but the heat emanating from the room was too much to bear. She remembered there was a fire extinguisher on the wall in the hallway, assuming the hallway was still there.

She stumbled out into the hall and moved to her right, using memory more than sight to find the extinguisher. It was closer than she realized and she almost slammed into it as she tripped over the rutted, smoldering carpeting.

Most of the glass on the metal box had been shattered, leaving just a few random, dangling shards, making the extinguisher hard to safely access. Jessie remembered the nightstick still shoved into the back of her pants and pulled it out, knocking the remaining pieces away. As she did, in the reflection of the largest shard still clinging to the box, she saw movement behind her.

She spun around, swinging the nightstick in front of her. It made firm contact with the right forearm of her father, who was clutching the knife in his hand as he dived at her. The weapon went flying. Now without the knife, he barreled into her, knocking her to the ground.

Jessie felt the wind leave her body as she first slammed to the floor and then felt his weight land on top of her. He looked down at her, apparently oblivious to the massive burn on the right side of his face and the blood pouring down his forehead from what looked like a chunk of drywall embedded in it.

"You betrayed the family, Junebug," he growled. "Just like your mother did. I wanted you to be the Thurman family savior. But it looks like you're going to be the sacrifice."

Now able to suck in some air, Jessie gripped the nightstick hard and swung it at his head. It made solid contact as she heard a sickening cracking sound. Yowling furiously, he yanked her to her feet and slammed her against the wall. The nightstick fell from her grip. She tried to shift into a position to knee him in the groin but he was too close and she couldn't get any leverage.

She saw his hand dart behind his back and pull something from his back pocket. He held it out in his palm for her to see. It was a switchblade. He flicked out the blade and raised it above his head, his eyes flashing. Then he repeated the same words he'd whispered in her ear twenty-three years ago as she sat strapped to a chair, about to watch her mother die.

"You have to see, little Junebug. You have to know the truth."

And then he brought the blade down, hard and fast, as the sound of a distant shot rang out.

CHAPTER THIRTY SIX

Jessie was still leaning against the wall but her father was no longer in front of her. She looked to her left and saw him lying on the ground, curled up in a ball. Then she looked to her right down the hall and saw someone with a gun aimed in their general direction. The smoke parted and she realized that it was Officer Tim Beatty.

"Don't move!" he shouted.

She had no intention of moving. But following his line of sight, she realized he wasn't yelling at her. She looked back to her left and saw her father slowly getting to his feet. His left arm hung limply at his side, a gaping, pulpy hole taking up most of his left shoulder.

He took a lurching step toward Jessie and another shot rang out. This time the bullet hit him in the left gut. Doubled over, he reeled backward, careening into the smoky haze of the open apartment door closest to him.

A couple of seconds later, as Beatty approached her, Jessie heard a shattering sound.

"Stay here," the officer said as he passed by her and into the mist of the unit where Xander had gone.

Unable to stand any longer, Jessie slid down the wall until she was in a sitting position. A few moments later, Beatty emerged from the apartment.

"He's gone," he said. "He threw a chair through a window and jumped out."

"Is he dead?" Jessie asked.

"I don't know. I don't see a body. The building's awning is below that unit so it might have broken his fall. But even if he survived, I can't imagine he'll get far with that stomach wound. How are you doing?"

"I'm okay." She winced. "You should go after him though, just to be safe. We can't let him get away."

"Okay," he said. "Are you sure you're good?"

She nodded and he started off down the hall, passing what remained of her apartment. That jogged her memory.

"Wait," she yelled, despite the pain. "Nettles. You have to get him. He's in my bedroom on the floor by the wall. He's hurt bad. My father cut his throat."

"What?" Beatty shouted as he ran into her unit, not waiting for an answer.

Jessie waited several seconds, trying to regain her strength. Eventually she managed to get to her feet and stumbled in the direction of her apartment. Just as she got there, Beatty emerged. Nettles was draped facedown over his right shoulder.

"Is he alive?" Jessie asked apprehensively.

"He has a pulse," Beatty said. "But I'm not sure for how much longer."

"I'll take care of him. You go after Thurman," she said.

"No way," Beatty argued. "We can't leave him here. It'll take the EMTs another ten minutes to get up here. He won't last that long. We have to go to them. And he's too big for you to carry."

"Let's get him downstairs," Jessie said, realizing he was right. "There has to be an ambulance here by now. If you can carry him, I'll get the doors."

Beatty nodded, though his silent grimace suggested it would be a struggle. He had been unconscious himself only minutes earlier and his head was probably screaming. They started down the corridor and were almost to the stairwell when the door shot open and three men in SWAT gear poured in.

"Nobody move!" the one in front yelled as he pointed his gun at them. "Identify yourselves."

Jessie looked over at Beatty, who seemed to be struggling to hold onto Nettles, much less speak. She decided to take the initiative.

"I'm Jessie Hunt, a criminal profiler for the department. These are Officers Beatty and Nettles of LAPD Central Station. This is my apartment building. These officers were assigned by Captain Roy Decker to protect me from my father, the serial killer Xander Thurman. He attacked us moments ago."

"I'm going to need ID," the SWAT officer barked, cutting her off.

"I will be happy to show you ID," she replied, keeping her tone calm but resolute. "But there are two more pressing issues. First, this officer was severely injured by Thurman. His throat was cut. He needs immediate medical attention. Second, Thurman jumped out of a window above the awning in front of the building. Officer Beatty shot him in the abdomen and shoulder and I think I fractured his skull with a nightstick. But he is still extremely dangerous. You should have men out there searching for him before he gets away."

Before the SWAT officer could reply, Beatty grunted in pain. Jessie looked over and could tell he was about to collapse.

"I need help," she demanded. "He can't hold Nettles any longer. Either I assist him or one of you does."

None of the SWAT officers moved so she did, stepping over to Beatty and helping him ease Nettles to the ground. The SWAT team's weapons remained trained on them.

"I'm sorry," Beatty huffed. "I thought I had him but I'm feeling woozy."

"It's okay. You were hit in the head. You probably have a concussion," she said before turning to the lead SWAT officer and pleading. "Can you please call for an EMT and ask someone downstairs to be on the lookout for a tall man in his fifties with a bullet hole in his gut?"

That seemed to turn the tide.

"Call it in," he ordered one of his cohorts. "EMT first, then the description. I'm going to assist here. Jeb—keep your weapon trained on both of these other two. Any sudden moves and they get it the kneecap."

Jessie took no offense, happy to suffer a blown out knee if it meant Nettles would survive.

Ten minutes later, Jessie sat in the back of an ambulance, watching an EMT attend to Beatty.

Nettles had been stabilized and immediately transported to Dignity Health Hospital, less than a five-minute drive away, where he would undergo emergency surgery. Units were out, canvassing the neighborhood for any sign of her father. So far, they'd come up empty and she feared it would stay that way.

The EMT who had treated her for her various burns from the explosion and what he suspected was a concussion came over.

"Your captain wants us to transport you both to the hospital. He's going to meet us there. We'll head out in a minute. Other officers are just checking to make there are no other injuries significant enough to make the trip with us."

Jessie nodded. As he stepped away, she watched the Crime Scene Unit van pull up, there to process the scene. The medical examiner would likely arrive soon to handle the bodies of Fred and Jimmy, two men who would be alive right now if she hadn't moved into this building. An ugly cocktail of guilt and dread was forming in her gut when her phone rang. It was Brady Bowen.

"Hey, Brady," she answered, impressed with how normal her voice sounded.

"Hi, Jessie. Sorry to bother you in the evening but I was hoping you could lend me a hand."

His voice sounded anxious but she got the distinct impression that he had no idea what her situation was. That was fine. If it meant shifting her attention away from what had just happened, she was more than willing to set aside her personal nightmare and focus on someone else's.

"How can I help?"

"We've definitely lost Gray Longworth," he said. "It's like he completely dropped off the grid. We've been going through his financials and found that he has a storage unit in Venice, not too far from his office. We're assigning a team to breach it in case he's holed up there. I'm going to join them."

"Okay," Jessie said, not sure where this was going. "It sounds like you've got things under control. What do you need me for?"

"Because one of the last communications Longworth sent before he went dark was a text to his wife saying it was her fault all of this was happening and she was going to regret how she's been treating him."

"That sounds ominous," Jessie said.

"I agree. I called her a little while ago. I didn't tell her what's going on. I said I just wanted to check in. She's at home and sounded like everything was normal. But I thought it might be worth it for someone to go over there and just check on her, maybe hang out for a bit until we get this resolved."

"And you want to send me?" Jessie asked, surprised. "You know I'm not a cop, right? Besides, we didn't exactly hit it off."

"I know. But I figured sending you would freak her out less than having a couple of uniformed officers stationed outside her house. Also, I can't get hold of Ryan. My calls keep going to his voicemail."

"He's getting in a workout," Jessie informed him. "He was feeling inadequate after Percival got the jump on him. He should be done soon. Are you sure that you're not just calling me because you think a chick would be better at comforting another chick?"

"First of all, that hurts," Brady said, mock offended. "I'm a modern man and would never make such archaic assumptions. Second, like you said, I've seen you two interact. There's no way I'd describe your manner as 'comforting.' I just need someone she knows to babysit her until we lock this down."

Jessie wanted to say no. The burns she'd suffered in the explosion needed attention and her head was still ringing slightly. But letting down an LAPD detective in need who was directly asking her for help felt like the wrong move. More importantly, if Gray Longworth ended up killing Eliza and she could have been there to help prevent it, she knew she'd never be able to forgive herself.

"Okay, I'll go."

"Thanks," he said, sounding genuinely grateful. "I'll see if Ryan can meet you when I finally reach him. I should warn you, it might be a few hours. We're a little short-handed for this raid. There was a massive pileup on the Pacific Coast Highway about an hour ago. There were multiple fatalities and half our units are there. Are you still okay with it?"

"I've already committed, Brady. I'd look pretty lame if I backed out now."

"Yes, you would. Thanks again. I'll keep you posted on how the raid goes."

He hung up without another word.

The EMT walked over, holding the forearm of a twenty-something woman who was limping slightly.

"We're taking this young lady as a precaution," he said, clearly annoyed. "She may have a sprained ankle. If you can hop in, Ms. Hunt, we'll head out."

"She can have my spot," Jessie told him. "Something's come up. I'll have to go to the hospital later."

"I don't think that's a great idea. Those burns could get infected and I'd like someone to evaluate your head. I'm almost positive you have a concussion. Besides, your captain would be pretty upset if you didn't show up."

"I appreciate the concern," Jessie said as she climbed out of the ambulance. "I promise to get checked out as soon as I finish this other thing. And I promise to call Decker to let him know what's up. You're off the hook."

"Somehow, I doubt that."

Considering she had no intention of calling the captain, the poor guy was probably right.

CHAPTER THIRTY SEVEN

Jessie almost drove off the road.

By the time she got to Pacific Palisades it was dark out. And with the limited lighting in the isolated, oceanside community, traversing the winding roads was challenging, even without a head injury. At least twice, she had to yank the wheel away from a canyon cliff.

She pulled up to the Longworth house and got out. As she walked to the front door, she texted both Ryan and Brady to let them know she'd arrived. She got no response from Ryan but Brady texted her back immediately.

His message read: *Venice storage unit was a bust. Checking office again. Running his credit cards to see if anything pops up. Sending a unit to meet you as a precaution. Stay alert.*

Staying alert was one thing. Doing anything about a potential threat was another. She was alone with a woman and her children in an isolated home without a sidearm. She didn't exactly project strength and security.

Fake it, Jessie. If you seem confident, she'll feel safe.

She knocked on the door. It took almost a minute for Eliza to answer. The second she did, Jessie knew she was drunk.

"What do you want?" Eliza asked, borderline hostile.

"Are your kids here?" Jessie asked before she could stop herself.

"No. They're at my mother's in Orange County. I needed a night off. In case you didn't notice, I've been under a little stress lately. Are you here to add to it?"

She wasn't slurring but Jessie could hear the mild effects of the liquid lubrication on her speech. She decided that if she was going to convince this woman to let her inside, the best course of action was deescalation.

"I hope not," she said mildly. "I'm actually here to help, if you'll let me. May I come in?"

'Promise not to interrogate me again?" Eliza asked.

"I promise." Jessie assured her.

"Fine," Eliza said and returned back down the hall, leaving Jessie to close and lock the door.

"Do you mind if we turn on your security system?" she asked as nonchalantly as she could.

"Shouldn't I be safe with the LAPD in my house?" Eliza called out from down the hall.

"I'm actually not a cop," Jessie told her. "And better safe than sorry, right?"

"I guess. The code is nine-eight-seven-six. I changed it after I kicked Gray out."

Jessie punched it in and followed the other woman down the hall into the living room, where Eliza was already plopped out on the couch with a glass and a bottle of vodka on the coffee table in front of her.

"You changed the code the night he left?" Jessie asked.

"Yup. Had a locksmith come out and change the locks too. Cost a pretty penny."

"Were you worried about your safety?"

"Nah," Eliza said dismissively. "I just didn't want him skulking back in and getting extra clothes or crashing on the couch or something. He deserved to muddle through in a hotel in the few things he managed to put in his suitcase."

"Is that why you didn't report the text he sent you this afternoon?" Jessie asked, sitting down in the hard-backed wooden chair opposite Eliza. "You don't view him as a threat, even after what happened to Penelope?"

"Maybe he was a threat to her, but not to me. You have to have passion for someone to do what was done to her. He doesn't have that for me anymore. In a weird way, I think we both loved Penny

191

more than each other. Anyway, I think his talk in that text of me being 'sorry' was mostly a financial threat."

"He's gone missing," Jessie told her flatly.

Eliza's vodka-dulled eyes perked up at that.

"Really?" she asked. "That's not very Gray-like. Is that why you're here—to protect me in case he comes to make me pay for my crime of feeling wronged?"

"Kind of, yeah. You're not concerned?"

"I wasn't until about ten seconds ago. But now you've got me a little freaked."

"Did he know the kids wouldn't be here tonight?" Jessie asked.

"Yeah. He called this morning and said he wanted to take them to dinner tonight. I told him they were at my mom's and he wasn't to go near them or I'd call the cops claiming attempted abduction."

"I'm sure he loved that," Jessie mused.

"Let's just say that his text was tame compared to what he said on the phone after I told him that," she admitted, then furrowed her brow. "What do you care anyway? The way you came at me the other day, it sounded like you wanted to throw me behind bars more than him."

"I was just doing my job, Mrs. Longworth," Jessie said. "Being sympathetic doesn't make you innocent. It's my job to follow all the leads, even if one of them is a woman who was betrayed by her husband and her best friend."

"Yeah, well, I guess you would know about betraying husbands," Eliza muttered.

"What do you mean?"

"Like I said, my mom lives in Orange County. When I told her about the case and mentioned your name, she knew exactly who you were—the wife of the cheating husband who tried to kill her. I would have thought you'd have understood where I was coming from a bit more."

"I do understand," Jessie insisted. "That's why I had to look at you harder—because I'm inclined to be sympathetic toward you."

"Yeah, well, what you call looking at me harder, I call being a bitch. But whatever."

"Look, I don't want to get into an argument now," Jessie said, trying to keep her cool even as her head throbbed, likely an aftereffect of the concussion. "Detective Brady asked me to come by until they locate your husband and keep an eye on things. That's what I'd like to do. Do you mind if I look around?"

"Suit yourself," Eliza said, refilling her half-empty glass.

Jessie walked around the entire main floor, checking that every door and window was locked. Then she did the same with the top floor. When she came back down, Eliza was in the kitchen, microwaving some popcorn.

"I was going to watch some crappy reality show," she said when she saw Jessie reenter the room. "You want to join me?"

"Maybe in a minute," Jessie said. "But from the outside, I thought this place was three stories. I only see two."

"The door to the lower floor is in the laundry room near the garage," Eliza said, pointing the way. "The house looks impressive with three stories and all. But the truth is that the lower level is more of a basement. We use it for storing supplies and stuff. It's a bit disappointing."

"Does that level have any access points? Doors? Windows?"

Eliza's face suddenly changed, losing the disinterested expression.

"Actually, there is a window facing the backyard."

"Have you checked to make sure it's locked?" Jessie asked.

"No. I haven't been down there in days."

"Okay," Jessie said, her heart sinking. "I'm going to go down and check it out. Do you have anything in the way of a fireplace poker or golf club I could borrow?"

"Gray's clubs are in the garage, right next to the door. But you don't really think he snuck in, do you?"

"Almost certainly not," Jessie said reassuringly. "But I'll take a peek just to make sure the window is locked and everything is in order."

"Maybe I should go down there with you," Eliza suggested, "to show you where everything is. It's easy to trip over stuff down there."

"No. My priority is keeping you safe. I'd prefer you stay up here. But maybe grab the phone and if you hear anything … unusual, call nine-one-one."

"What about the whole 'strength in numbers' thing?" Eliza asked. "You might need me."

"That numbers thing may be true in general but when one of those people is vodka-soaked, the strength tends to be minimized. No offense."

"Offense kind of taken," Eliza replied.

"Sorry," Jessie said, though it was clear to both of them that she wasn't.

"I have to tell you, Ms. Hunt, you are seriously crushing my buzz."

Jessie didn't reply but instead walked down the hall to the garage, grabbed a nice pitching wedge from Gray's golf bag, and opened the laundry door. Eliza poked her head out from the living room and waved the phone to indicate she was ready.

Jessie nodded, opened the door that led from the laundry room to the lower level, turned on the flickering light, and took her first step down the rickety wooden stairwell.

Chapter Thirty Eight

J essie wasn't sure the stairs would hold.

Each step creaked loudly, warning anyone potentially down below of her presence and making her fear the wood would simply crack, sending her hurtling toward the floor.

Despite her misgivings, the stairs did not collapse. When she got to the bottom, she turned on the light switch attached to a wooden support beam. The light it offered was an unimpressive, dull, flickering yellow which sent weak, unpenetrating rays through what turned out to be one large, unfurnished room filled with boxes, supplies, and furniture. She noticed that the unsteady flickering of the light bulb exacerbated the pain in her head.

With the pitching wedge held behind her shoulder like a baseball bat, Jessie approached the one window in the place, along the back wall which abutted the hillside. She walked over and saw that the single latch-style lock was in place.

She put down the gold club and tried to push the widow open, just in case. It didn't budge. She quickly grabbed the club again and spun around facing the room. Just because the window was locked now didn't mean someone hadn't come in earlier and done it themselves.

She moved methodically around the rest of the room, checking behind large boxes and the water heater. The room seemed unoccupied. She was about to return up the stairs when she noticed that what appeared initially to be a decorative design along the far wall was actually the narrow door of a small closet.

She moved toward it slowly, trying to breathe silently so that she could hear if there was anyone doing the same behind the door. When she was close, she grabbed the handle with her left hand while maintaining a strong grip on the golf club with her right. Without pausing to reconsider, she yanked it open and stepped back.

There was no one there. In fact, the closet was sparsely populated by an old vacuum cleaner, a few wobbly lamps, an old broom, and a battered-looking, soft-sided suitcase in the back corner.

Jessie was about to close the door when her eyes fell again on the suitcase. She noticed that it was bulging slightly in the middle, as if there was something inside it. That wasn't unusual. Jessie shoved duffel bags and backpacks inside her luggage to save space in her apartment.

But something about the shape of the bulge felt familiar in a way she couldn't quite place. She used a dangling string to turn on the overhead light in the closet. Then she pulled a tissue out of her pocket and used it to slowly unzip the suitcase.

Inside the luggage was a tub of bleach. On the front was the name Green Clean, the same eco-friendly brand that Ryan had said was used to clean the knife that killed Penelope; the brand he'd said was hard to find, even in this neighborhood.

Jessie involuntarily gripped the club tighter. She closed the door and started back up the stairs, trying to calculate the odds that this particular brand of bleach just happened to be stored in a closet in the home of people suspected in the murder of their neighbor.

She stopped midway up the stairs to see if her phone had any service so she could text Brady and Ryan about her discovery. She wasn't surprised to find there were no bars. When she got to the top, she half-expected to find Gray Longworth standing there with a bloody kitchen knife in his hand. But there was no one.

She glanced around the laundry room, looking for another tub of the Green Clean bleach. None was immediately visible. She opened the cupboard above the washer and found nothing there either.

Increasingly unsettled and feeling mildly nauseated from the ache in her head, she headed back down the hall to the living room where she found Eliza standing in the kitchen, munching on popcorn in a bowl on the counter with one hand while still holding the phone in the other.

"Everything okay?" she asked. "Do I need to call nine-one-one or was the window locked?"

"It was," Jessie said. "Nothing to worry about on that front."

"Then why are you still holding the golf club?" Eliza asked, nodding at the pitching wedge Jessie was still clasping tightly.

"Oh. I figured it would have to do in place of a gun. You don't mind, do you?"

"No," Eliza said as she put the phone back in its cradle. "But just be careful where you swing it. Our art isn't expensive but I'm still fond of it."

"No problem," Jessie said as a series of thoughts began to bombard the edges of her brain. "Do you think I could wash my hands? They got a little dirty down there. And I'd love some ibuprofen if you have it. My head is killing me."

Eliza handed her a cup and a bottle of pills sitting on the counter, then waved her in the direction of the kitchen sink with a faux ostentatious flourish. Jessie walked over, rested the pitching wedge on the ground against the cabinet, and turned the faucet on. She rubbed her hands into a soapy lather as the sound of the water worked as a kind of quiet noise, helping her organize her pinballing thoughts.

The bleach is hard to find but the victim's next door neighbors have it. They didn't keep it in the laundry room but stuffed it in a suitcase in a little-used closet in a rarely accessed basement-style room.

She recalled her initial questioning of Eliza Longworth, when the woman had said that Gray didn't even know how to do the laundry.

How likely is it that he'd even know they had bleach, much less where to find it?

Then she recalled how Eliza had said, only minutes earlier, that she'd changed the locks and the security code to the house the same day that she'd discovered the affair, when Penelope was still alive. The bleach knife-cleaning hadn't happened until the following morning, when Gray didn't even have access to the house.

A creeping sense of unease settled over Jessie. As she dried her hands, she glanced over at Eliza, who seemed oblivious to her, tossing popcorn in her mouth as she watched one of the *Real Housewives* shows.

Just then, her phone pinged multiple times in row.

"Whoa," she said, pulling it from her pocket.

"That's probably all of your messages coming in at once," Eliza said without turning around. "For some reason, cell reception is best in the kitchen. That's why I spend half my time in here."

"Good to know," Jessie said as she scrolled through the five messages that had all arrived at once. She saw that she had multiple voicemails as well.

The first text was from Captain Decker, reaming her out for not being at the hospital to meet him. The second was from Ryan, saying that he would meet her at her apartment in twenty minutes. Apparently he didn't know what had happened when he sent it. The third text was from Decker again, threatening to suspend her if she didn't respond to him ASAP. The fourth was from Ryan, saying he'd just talked to Brady and was on his way to Eliza's house to help keep an eye on things. He made no mention of the incident at the apartment, meaning he either didn't know or had decided to let it go. The final text was from Brady. It read:

Found Longworth. Was drunk in a bar. Phone was dead. No threat to wife. You can stand down.

"You're a popular girl," Eliza said, glancing over at her.

Jessie gulped silently, realizing that the woman standing in front of her was almost certainly not what she seemed. She tried to respond casually.

"Maybe too popular," she said, noticing a slight quiver in her voice. "It seems my apartment was broken into tonight."

"Oh, that sucks," Eliza said, turning to face her. She looked more clear-headed than she had earlier.

"Thanks. Bad news for me. But I have good news for you."

"What's that?"

"Detective Bowen texted. It looks like your husband isn't after you after all. They found him in a bar, drowning his sorrows in a glass. His phone had died, which is why they couldn't get hold of him."

"That's reassuring," Eliza said insincerely. "Then I'm safe?"

"It appears you are. So that means I can get out of your hair. You can go back to the *Real Housewives* and I can go deal with my apartment break-in."

Eliza nodded. She was no longer looking at Jessie but staring blankly off in the distance. After a moment, she returned her attention to Jessie. Her non-popcorn hand rested on a dish towel on the counter.

"You know, don't you?" she said, her voice a mix of apprehension and acceptance.

Jessie studied her without speaking. Eliza looked alert, despite the multiple vodkas. Her eyes were fixed on Jessie, who noticed that there seemed to be a bump under the dish towel, as if there was something resting underneath it on the counter. Glancing over, she saw that the cutlery block in the corner was one knife short.

She looked back at Eliza, realizing that her next words could change both their lives.

CHAPTER THIRTY NINE

"Know what?' she asked, trying to keep her voice breezy even as her pulse quickened.

Eliza seemed to be debating how to respond. She had stopped eating popcorn and her right hand still pressed on the dish towel with the suspicious bump below it. Finally, she replied, with a tone of resignation.

"As soon as you said you were going to check the lower level of the house, I knew I had a problem," she said matter-of-factly. "I hoped that if I went down there with you, I could distract you. But you were so concerned for my safety, I had to let it go and hope you were sloppy. But you weren't, were you?"

"What are you talking about, Eliza?" Jessie asked innocently, forcing herself not to glance over at the pitching wedge leaning against the counter a few feet away. "I said there was no one down there."

She knew this stalling wouldn't work much longer but she needed a few seconds to formulate a plan before Eliza got direct and things escalated.

"You have to understand," Eliza insisted, ignoring Jessie's protestations, her voice rising in volume and intensity. "It was never my plan for it to go down like it did. I really thought I could move past what happened. But then I saw her and she wasn't as contrite as I thought she should have been. She should have oozed remorse. She knew what I've been through. You know what I mean, Ms. Hunt?"

"I do, Eliza," Jessie said, trying to compensate for the other woman's obvious angst by acting as calm as possible.

"When I was in college," Eliza continued, clearly not assuaged, "I was … victimized. Penny helped me through it. She was my rock. So to then have the person who most understood my vulnerabilities callously disregard them? It really stung. I mean, that doesn't even begin to describe it. It was crushing. It was like an earthquake only I could feel. Does that make any sense at all?"

"It does," Jessie soothed. "I get it. Remember, I've been where you were."

Eliza answered, though it wasn't clear she had even heard Jessie.

"But I didn't feel the appropriate shame or penitence coming from her," she said, her voice getting dangerously quiet. "And, I don't know, this fury just erupted in me and I gave in to it."

"You're admitting to me that you killed Penelope," Jessie said, deciding that being direct would have to replace being cagey as a tactic.

"Might as well, right?" Eliza said, forthcoming in a way that Jessie found disquieting. "We both know you saw the fancy, eco-friendly, super-expensive, order-it-from-Amazon, easy-to-trace bleach. And who keeps bleach in their basement but not their laundry room, right? I wanted to throw it out but I knew you guys had officers watching me. Even if I dumped the whole thing down the drain, I'd still have to dispose of the empty tub somehow. No one noticed it when they did that rush search of the house the other day. But I knew they'd be back. Still, I hoped that I could do it in a few days, when everything settled down and no one was following me around."

"So you cleaned off the knife and decided to toss it on the trail to make Gray look guilty?"

The frenzied look in Eliza's eyes seemed to fade a bit as she recalled the particulars of how it had played out.

"I wish I could say I planned all that out," she admitted. "After I killed Penny—it's weird to say that out loud—I took the knife home to clean the prints off and check that I didn't have blood on me. I was surprisingly clean considering what I'd just done.

"I was actually coming back for the yoga lesson, hoping to both use it as an alibi and put the knife back in the cutlery block before

Beth got there. Looking back, it's strange how cool and collected I was in the moment. It was like I was watching myself from above, like it wasn't really me doing all that stuff. Is that what usually happens when you kill someone? This is my first time."

"I don't know," Jessie said softly, unsure how to respond, uncertain what might set the other woman off.

"Anyway," Eliza said, resuming her story as if she was telling a girlfriend about her day, "then I saw Gray's car on the way over and realized he must have gone for a run. That's when I thought it was worth a shot to throw the knife on the trail. I didn't know which route he took but it would look suspicious either way, right?"

Her voice was clear, but she was talking fast, with a manic edge.

"Right," Jessie agreed, trying to slow everything down. "So it really was just a crime of passion? You didn't plan it all out?"

"God no," she said, genuinely shocked at the idea. "I was winging everything. I had to pray that Beth didn't see me come around from the back of the house when she was driving up. I caught a break there. And I lucked out in that there were so many other suspects—Penny's slimy husband, my slimy husband, other guys she'd slept with over the years. I started to think I might actually get away with it. You know, so it could eat at me silently for the rest of my life."

"And now?"

"I think you know what now," Eliza replied, her voice suddenly steely as her hand tightened the item beneath the dish towel. "I can't have this come out. I can't go to jail and be taken away from my kids."

Jessie started to speak but Eliza held out her free hand. She wasn't done.

"I was thinking while you were downstairs. And it occurred to me that if you were killed with a knife and I was badly injured as well, the whole path of the investigation might change. I could tell the police that it was a masked assailant. Then all the talk of the killer being someone she knew would go away. They'd start looking at local break-ins and random violent crimes in the area. It could actually be a lifesaver; my life, of course."

"But here's the problem with that," Jessie said carefully, trying to keep things conversational so Eliza's grip on the big knife under the towel didn't get any firmer. "It won't work."

"How can you be sure?" Eliza demanded.

"You're not thinking clearly. I understand—you're in a desperate situation and you're looking for any way out. But, Eliza, these detectives are smart. They're not going to just accept the theory that it was a random attack. They'll look at the angles of the knife wounds in me. They'll be able to tell that yours were self-inflicted. Detective Hernandez will figure out that I discovered something in this house that set you off. He knows me."

"He certainly seems as if he'd like to get to know you better," Eliza said, her tone barbed.

"Let's keep the focus on your future, Eliza," Jessie said firmly. "Because you can still have one."

"How do you figure? I slaughtered my best friend." Her voice cracked as she said it.

"In a fit of passion," Jessie reminded her. "Then you tried to cover it up after the fact. That's all true. But that doesn't have to be the end of the story. If you go to trial, your attorney could likely make a compelling case for temporary insanity. Your best friend of twenty-five years was having an affair with your husband. You snapped. Anyone could understand that. I guarantee you I could. I wanted to wring my husband's neck. And had he not already murdered his mistress, I might have. You could get off."

"I think we both know that's unlikely," Eliza said, though her voice suggested she wasn't totally convinced.

"Maybe, maybe not," Jessie said, keeping the pressure on. "You never know with juries. Even if they convict you, it might be on a lesser charge. That's not unusual with crimes of passion. The prosecutor might not even want to go to trial because you're a sympathetic defendant. They might worry about jury nullification and offer a plea. There's a reasonable chance that you could get out in a few years and still be around to watch your children grow up."

"But..." Eliza said, sensing there was a "but."

"But not if you pick up the knife you're hiding under that towel. Then you're attempting to commit a second murder. And whether you succeed or not, you'll be caught. And no one will buy the 'wronged wife' defense anymore. You'll just be someone who went after a member of law enforcement to cover your ass—no mitigating circumstances. They'll throw the book at you."

She sensed Eliza turning it over in her head and continued, wanting to keep the momentum going.

"If you're successful in killing me, and you won't be," she said with a confidence she didn't feel, "you'll go to jail for decades. Gray, the man who betrayed you, will raise your children and they will have their own babies before you ever get out. And if you did actually kill a criminal profiler for the Los Angeles Police Department, you'd probably be looking at the death penalty, even in California. If I were you, I'd pick door number one, step away from the knife, turn around, and get on your knees. It's the only way to see your family again soon from anywhere but behind glass."

Eliza stared at her for a long time, her hand frozen on the towel, her eyes darting about madly. When she finally spoke, it was with a certainty that Jessie found disconcerting.

"I think you're messing with me, Ms. Hunt," she said. "I think you're painting a worst-case-scenario picture that might never play out. There's no reason the intruder story can't work. Thanks to your tip, I'll make sure to give myself convincing wounds, ones too awful for anyone to think I would perpetrate them myself. I'll..."

In that moment, Jessie came to a decision. It was clear that Eliza had made her choice, even if she hadn't yet acted on it. There was no point in waiting for her to make the first move. This might be Jessie's only chance to surprise the unhinged woman in front of her.

So while Eliza was mid-sentence, Jessie reached for the golf club. Unfortunately, she moved too fast and instead of grabbing it, she accidentally bumped the handle, knocking the club over and sending it sliding noisily across the kitchen floor.

Eliza stared at her open-mouthed for a fraction of a second. Then she grabbed the knife.

CHAPTER FORTY

J essie didn't wait.

She leapt at Eliza as she raised the butcher knife above her head. The other woman was just starting to pull the blade downward when Jessie made contact, slamming her against the kitchen counter with her shoulder as she blocked the descending knife with her forearm.

The force sent Eliza stumbling back before Jessie could try to grab the weapon from her. As the woman found her footing, Jessie looked around desperately, ignoring her throbbing head. The golf club was near Eliza's feet, useless. She had no weapon. She was defenseless.

The only thing in reaching distance was the popcorn bowl. She grabbed it and tossed what was left inside at Eliza. As the fluffy kernels bounced off her body, the other woman smiled at the absurdity of the situation.

"This is a hell of a thing," she marveled, holding the long knife up near her face. "I wouldn't have predicted this scenario at the start of my week."

"Eliza, don't do this," Jessie pleaded as she grabbed the bowl by the edges, with the domed bottom facing away from her. "Is this how you want your children to see you? If you don't drop that knife, you're not just destroying your own life. You're ruining their futures too."

"It's a little late to be worried about that, don't you think? I'm committed."

With that, she started forward again, knife raised. She was smaller than Jessie but with the build of a former athlete who still kept in shape, she wasn't going to be easily subdued.

Jessie didn't have time to remember all the self-defense training she'd learned at the FBI, but one rule did pop into her head. Let your attacker make the first move and counter it. As Eliza barreled toward her, she held steady.

Let her get out of position.

Eliza again lifted the knife high and plunged it down sharply. Jessie raised the bowl to block the blow. The blade connected with the bottom of the bowl and slid off harmlessly to the side. Instead of retreating, Jessie continued to thrust the bowl forward forcefully. The base of the bowl slammed squarely into Eliza's face, nailing her hard in the mouth and the nose.

She looked more shocked than hurt but Jessie took advantage of the moment to whack her a second time in the face with the bowl. Then, with all the strength she could muster, she yanked the bowl down, making contact with both the knife handle and Eliza's right wrist. The weapon popped out of her hand and tumbled to the ground.

Jessie didn't wait to see what had happened. As Eliza tried to track the location of the knife, Jessie swung the popcorn bowl up again, squarely connecting with the other woman's jaw before she could raise her arms to protect herself.

Eliza staggered backward, clearly stunned. Jessie stayed aggressive, tossing away the bowl and taking one step forward before lifting her leg and kicking the other woman in the stomach. Eliza flew backward and slammed into the far wall of the kitchen before collapsing to the ground.

Jessie approached her carefully. Eliza was conscious but obviously disoriented. Jessie quickly grabbed her by the ankles, yanking her into a prone position on her back. As she dropped the last few feet, Eliza's head bounced hard on the kitchen floor. Jessie ignored it and flipped her over. Then she dropped down, pinning her knee in the small of the other woman's back.

She looked on the counter for anything to help her restrain Eliza and saw a blender in the corner. She yanked the cord out of the wall, snagged some kitchen shears from the cutlery block, and cut the cord. She seized Eliza's wrists and tied them behind her back.

When she was she sure the cord was fastened tight and without removing her knee from Eliza's back, she pulled her phone out.

"Hey look," she said though breathing heavily, "the reception *is* better in the kitchen."

Then she called Ryan.

CHAPTER FORTY ONE

Jessie had held back the tears for so long that when they finally came, they wouldn't stop.

It was only when the graveside service was over and they were leaving the cemetery that she finally started to gain some control.

The weather was still chilly in Las Cruces in March and there was a light dusting of snow on the ground. As she walked back to the limo that would take her to the memorial reception at Pa's favorite bar, Kat Gentry and Ryan Hernandez fell into step beside her. No one spoke for a while.

"I've never seen so many rickety old law enforcement types all together at once," Ryan finally said. "I thought maybe oxygen machines and wheelchairs would have been provided."

Jessie smiled weakly at his attempt at humor. She appreciated the effort.

"They *are* a mature group," she finally managed to reply as they got to the limo. "We'll have to keep a close eye on them at the bar. Some of these folks have trouble standing upright when they're sober. Drunk could be ugly."

Jessie was a little surprised at how emotional she'd gotten as her parents were lowered into the ground. She couldn't remember truly losing it like this in all the years she'd lived with them. There had always been that tough outer shell surrounding her, ever since she'd seen her mother murdered. It was like someone had shut off the part of her that allowed her to truly feel grief because if she ever did, it would be too overwhelming to process.

She assumed it would be that way today too. After all, the last few days had been a whirlwind of activity which forced her to keep her emotions in check. First, she had to help wrap up the Penelope Wooten murder case, including all the reports she had to fill out on her capture of Eliza Longworth.

In between were several hospital visits to get her head checked out after that altercation and the one at her apartment with her father. Her burns had been treated and her concussion diagnosis confirmed. She'd been ordered to take it easy for a while and come back for an all-clear before resuming work. That worked out because she had another job to do: find a new place to live. Right now she was living out of a hotel room.

All of it had been so time consuming and attention depleting that she simply hadn't had any truly quiet moments to deal with what had happened to her family or think about the man who had done this to them. But in the cemetery earlier, with no responsibilities other than to say goodbye to the two people who had raised her—had saved her—after her world fell apart, she couldn't keep the walls up any longer.

She tried not to punish herself, remembering what Pa had always told her: they knew the risk they had taken adopting her all those years ago. They knew who her birth father was and that he might one day find her. They knew that they were putting their own lives in danger by joining them with hers. The fact that the danger materialized over two decades later didn't change that.

Still, she'd allowed herself to think the threat—at least to them—had passed. She never imagined that Xander would seek vengeance by killing two retirees living out their golden years. But they had eventually paid the price for getting close to her, just as Fred the security guard and Jimmy the doorman had paid the price just for working in the building where she lived. The funerals for those two men would be early next week.

As they rode to the bar, Jessie wondered how she'd hold up. The families of those men didn't know that their deaths were connected to her and wouldn't harbor any resentment to her when she offered her condolences. But *she* would know.

Officer Nettles was another story. He was on the road to recovery—the doctors had told him that he would be able to speak again in weeks and likely return to the job in a few months. But his wife was furious at having almost lost him while protecting Jessie and had prohibited her from visiting him in the hospital. She understood.

Captain Decker was going easy on her, giving her two weeks off to recover physically and emotionally. Having been attacked twice in the same night by murderers gave her a bit of a pass for not meeting him at the hospital or calling in, though Ryan warned her she might not get too many more.

There were other issues she'd need to attend to, even if she wasn't working. Highest on the list was determining what had happened to her father after he jumped out the window of her apartment complex.

He had been in bad shape, with gunshot wounds to the abdomen and shoulder, multiple burns from the explosions he'd set, and, she was fairly certain, a fractured skull. And since he couldn't go to a hospital in the area to get treated, he was likely recuperating underground.

Decker seemed convinced he was dead. That belief was based on detectives finding a badly burned body about a mile away at the edge of a homeless encampment. It was too charred for identification but the M.E. indicated that the man was in his fifties and had gunshot shrapnel in left shoulder and ribs. The approximate time of death correlated with when Xander was shot.

But Jessie knew better. Xander Thurman would not have ended up burned to death at the hands of a homeless man. He would have created a cover story and gone deep underground so that he could recover and regroup without police searching for him. He would lie low until the pressure was off and he was strong enough to accomplish his mission. Jessie was pretty sure that mission was making her pay for rejecting him; for not joining him in his grand undertaking to thin the herd and rid the world of unworthy souls. He might be out of commission for a while, but not forever.

They were still trying to determine exactly how he'd found her. One of the tech folks had uncovered footage of what looked like him at the El Paso airport the morning Jessie flew back to L.A. If he'd seen her enter the terminal, even if he couldn't go in himself without a ticket, it wouldn't have been hard to narrow down her possible destinations.

How he'd found her apartment complex was still a mystery, however. Jessie knew she'd have to answer that question if she was going to feel secure wherever she next planted roots. And she also decided that her new home must include one other essential element. It had to be a place where no one else was put at risk like Fred and Jimmy had been.

In between home-hunting, she had one other major responsibility. She had to provide testimony in anticipation of Eliza Longworth's preliminary hearing, at which she would be charged with counts of murder and attempted murder, among other things.

Brady Bowen, who had apologized more times than she could count for putting her "in harm's way," had agreed that if Eliza had just turned herself in instead of attacking Jessie, she might have been out in under a decade and seen both her kids graduate from high school.

Now she'd languish in prison for decades, stuck with the knowledge that the man who'd betrayed her trust was raising their kids. But she had made her choice and Jessie's reservoir of sympathy for her was mostly empty.

At the bar, seemingly every retired law enforcement officer in southern New Mexico wanted to offer a toast to Bruce and Janine Hunt. If Jessie had partaken of them all, she wouldn't make it outside upright, much less to the airport for her evening flight back to L.A. So after the first couple of shots, she switched to mineral water, as did Kat and Ryan.

Every song that played was one of Bruce's or Janine's personal favorites. A few times, especially during Patsy Cline's rendition of "Crazy," she caught Ryan looking at her when he thought she wouldn't notice. She found herself doing the same thing to him and realized that at some point, when her life settled down, she'd need to figure out exactly what was going on there.

Thoughts of Ryan disappeared as the next song started to play. It was "Don't Worry Be Happy" by Bobby McFerrin. A wave of memories suddenly cascaded over her all at once. She pictured Pa offering her a hand up after she'd fallen while skiing on a bunny slope. She saw Ma waiting at the front door when she got home from school, holding out a mug of hot chocolate topped with a massive mound of whipped cream. She remembered both of them rushing into her room when she would scream at bedtime and staying there all night long, scrunched up on her small bed, so that they were the first thing she saw when she woke up in the morning. She turned away from Kat and Ryan and used her sleeve to wipe at the tears rolling down her cheeks.

They had been there about an hour when Kat got a call. Jessie couldn't hear what it was about in the noisy pub but she saw her friend's face fall and knew it was something bad. Kat waved to get the bartender's attention.

"Is there an extra room where I can take this call?" she shouted. "It's law enforcement business."

"Isn't everything here?" the guy yelled with a grin, before adding, "You can use the office in the back."

Kat thanked him and motioned for Jessie and Ryan to follow her. The three of them made their way down the hall to the back office and closed the door, which somewhat muffled the shouts and cheers from the front.

"What is it?" Jessie asked.

Kat held up a finger and pushed a button on her phone, which she rested on a desk.

"Administrator Phelan, can you hear me?" she asked.

"I can," said an older male voice.

"Administrator, I've put you on speaker. I'm here with LAPD Detective Ryan Hernandez and criminal profiler Jessie Hunt. Guys—Paul Phelan is the supervising administrator for the NRD facility. He's my boss. Go ahead, Administrator—you said you had a priority update."

"That is correct," Phelan said. "I've just sent you security footage of an incident that occurred less than thirty minutes ago. It seems that Bolton Crutchfield has escaped from the high-security NRD annex."

"What?" Kat demanded. "How is that possible?"

"It appears that he had assistance. You can review the footage but the short version is that four members of our unit interior security staff were killed. One more was found unconscious in the break room. Two exterior guards were also killed and one other is in critical condition. In addition, all the other prisoners were set free by Crutchfield."

"This is Detective Hernandez, Administrator," Ryan interjected. "Have resources been deployed to retrieve the prisoners?"

"Many resources, Detective. We have LAPD, Sheriff's Department, Highway Patrol, and even FBI out there right now. Unfortunately, so far only one prisoner has been retrieved."

"Crutchfield did that on purpose," Jessie said, her mind already revving up. "He wants police resources dispersed, having to hunt for multiple escapees instead of just him."

"Well, it's working so far," Phelan said. "There's been no sign of him since he left the facility. How soon can you get back here, Officer Gentry?"

"We were booked on a flight this evening," Kat said. "But I'll go to the airport now and see if I can get on an earlier one."

"Please see that you do. I'll apprise you of any relevant updates in the interim."

He hung up without another word.

"I'm going with you," Jessie said.

"No, you should stay here for the rest of the wake. There's nothing you can do back there right now."

"Let me at least see the security footage," Jessie insisted. "Maybe there are some useful clues on it."

Kat pulled up the footage on her phone and placed it on the desk where all three of them could see it. There was no audio. It opened with a wide shot of the main security station at the center of the secure unit. There were three officers at the desk. After a few seconds, Ernie Cortez, the massive, genial guard who was always hitting on Jessie, appeared onscreen.

He was holding something in his right hand as he stepped behind the officer on the right, studying a monitor in front of him. In one swift, deft motion Ernie pulled out the item, which was now revealed to be a hunting knife, and slit the officer's throat. The female officer next to him looked over just in time to see Ernie plunge the knife into her forehead. As she fell back, the third guard, just to her left, stood up, reaching for his weapon. But before he could get it out of his holster, Ernie was on him, grabbing his gun hand while smashing the guard's head backward against the station desk's wall. The two men tumbled out of frame so that only their legs were visible. After a few seconds, the other guard's legs stopped moving.

Ernie returned to the frame, where he pulled the knife out of the female officer's head and moved around the desk to stand near where one of the hall spokes met the central area. He hid there, unmoving, with his back pressed to the wall. A few seconds later, a fourth guard appeared from that direction with a perplexed look on his face. He was clearly confused by the lack of any staff at the security station.

As he passed Ernie, the larger man wrapped his left arm around the guard's arms while simultaneously cutting his throat. The guard dropped to the floor, writhing slightly. Ernie, oblivious, walked around to the security desk and typed in something on one of the keyboards. Then he disappeared from the frame again.

About a minute later he reemerged. Only this time he wasn't alone. Bolton Crutchfield was with him. As Ernie left again, apparently releasing the other prisoners, Crutchfield got into the uniform of the guard who had tried to go for his gun. As he changed, he spoke. Jessie could see other prisoners milling about in the background, listening intently to what he was saying.

Then Bolton Crutchfield turned and faced the very camera they were watching him on. He smiled up at them and waved. Then he turned and focused his attention on the first guard whose throat had been slit and who was still sitting slumped over in his chair.

Jessie couldn't see what he was doing. But after about thirty seconds, he turned back around and faced the camera. He was holding something. As he approached the camera, he held it up.

It was a clipboard with a single white sheet of paper attached. On it, he had written something. As he brought it closer, Jessie realized that he had written the message in the blood of the guard, using his index finger as the pen.

He held up the paper right in front of the camera so that the words were clearly visible, though they dripped slightly.

Jessie looked at it, unable to stop the suddenly bubbling cauldron of fear from twisting her insides into knots. She extended her arms to brace herself on the desk, afraid that she might topple over without assistance. Ryan gripped her shoulders in support as she looked over at Kat, whose face mirrored the horror she felt.

The message read:

Be seeing you, Miss Jessie.

After holding the sign up for what felt like an eternity, Bolton Crutchfield dropped the clipboard to floor, gave them one last, chilling smile, and disappeared from sight.

Now Available for Pre-Order!

THE PERFECT SMILE
(A Jessie Hunt Psychological Suspense Thriller—Book Four)

In THE PERFECT SMILE (Book #4), criminal profiler Jessie Hunt, 29, fresh from the FBI Academy, is assigned a disturbing new case: a woman in her 30s has been murdered after using a dating website for her affairs with married men.

Had she gotten too close to one of the married men?

Was she the victim of blackmail? Of a stalker?

Or was there some far more nefarious motive at stake?

The list of suspects takes Jessie into wealthy, manicured neighbor-hoods, behind the veil of seemingly perfect lives, lives which are actually rotten to the core. The killer, she realizes, must lie behind one of these fake, plastic smiles.

Jessie must plumb the depths of his psychosis as she tries to both catch a killer and hold her own fragile psyche together—with her own murderous father on the loose, willing to stop at nothing until he kills her.

A fast-paced psychological suspense thriller with unforgettable characters and heart-pounding suspense, THE PERFECT SMILE is book #4 in a riveting new series that will leave you turning pages late into the night.

Book #5 in the Jessie Hunt series will be available soon.

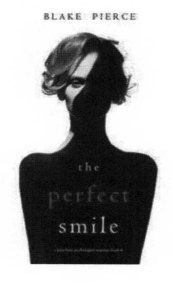

THE PERFECT SMILE
(A Jessie Hunt Psychological Suspense Thriller—Book Four)

Did you know that I've written multiple novels in the mystery genre? If you haven't read all my series, click the image below to download a series starter!

Made in the USA
Middletown, DE
23 May 2021